THE ENIGMA OF A WIDOW

LINDA RAE SANDE

Twisted Teacup
PUBLISHING

The Enigma of a Widow

V1.4

Cover photograph © Period Images.com

Cover art by KGee Designs.

http://www.lindaraesande.com

ISBN: 978-0-9964433-9-5

Library of Congress Control Number: 2017900217

Twisted Teacup Publishing, Cody, Wyoming

PRINTED IN THE UNITED STATES OF AMERICA

In memory of my grandmother—she would have made an excellent spy

The Charity of a Viscount

The Cousins of the Aristocracy

The Promise of a Gentleman

The Pride of a Gentleman

The Holidays of the Aristocracy

The Christmas of a Countess

The Knot of a Knight

The Heirs of the Aristocracy

The Angel of an Astronomer

The Puzzle of a Bastard

The Choice of a Cavalier

The Bargain of a Baroness

The Jewel of an Earl's Heir

The Vixen of a Viscount

The Honor of an Heir

The Ladies of the Aristocracy

The Lady of a Grump

The Lady of a Sultan

Beyond the Aristocracy

The Pleasure of a Pirate

The Making of a Mistress

The Bride of a Baronet

The Lyon's Den (Dragonblade Publishing)

The Courage of a Lyon

Stella of Akrotiri

Origins

Deminon

Diana

PROLOGUE

June 15, 1816 (The Year of No Summer)

A snowflake danced about in the chill, its twisted path to the ground made so by the man who blew air between his lips each time it seemed determined to continue its descent. With the man's next breath, the crystalline structure twirled about and then disappeared.

The man frowned and stared at where the snowflake should have been. He continued staring until the shout of a nearby costermonger had him giving a start. His cane, a silver-topped length of mahogany polished to a high shine, nearly fell from his right hand before he steadied it with the other.

Dammit.

Adonis Truscott took a steadying breath and grimaced when another snowflake passed in front of his face, its path downward nearly straight. Glancing about, as if to ascertain his whereabouts, he wondered at how long he had allowed the falling snow to capture his attention. How long he had stared at the space where the snowflake had disappeared. How long he had stood on the pavement next to the haberdashery in Old Bond Street.

In the effort to view his chronometer, he found his

gloved hands so stiff, they could barely grasp the metallic disk, let alone press the button that would open the lid.

"You won't find a hackney this time of the day," a male voice said from behind him.

Turning to discover the owner of the voice, Adonis regarded the rather tall man and gave a nod. "No, I don't suppose so," he agreed with a sigh, realizing he was speaking to the owner of the haberdashery. He had been in the shop earlier to purchase the red woolen scarf that was now wrapped around his neck and dusted with snowflakes. At that moment, he couldn't recall how he had made his way to Old Bond Street. He thought he had ridden his horse, but it was possible he had arrived in a hackney. Or perhaps a town coach.

"Come back into the shop. You must be freezing."

Adonis nodded. "Just for a moment," he agreed as he turned to follow the proprietor. He was nearly through the green gloss painted door when a female voice called out.

"Donald!"

Stiffening where he stood, Adonis suddenly remembered exactly how he had arrived in Old Bond Street. "Seems my ride has remembered where she left me," he said to the shop owner. He gave the man a short bow and leaned on his cane as he turned and directed his attention to the town coach that was now parked in front of the haberdashery. The matched greys in front of the equipage snorted clouds of white as they stomped their impatience. Given the chill in the air, Adonis found he couldn't blame them.

Despite how his leg protested climbing into the town coach, Adonis was able to negotiate the high step and take a seat in the stiff squabs. Although several hot coals glowed in a brazier between the seats, the inside of the coach wasn't much warmer than outside, that is, until the driver could get the door shut.

"Where have you *been?*" Persephone Craven demanded from beneath the quilt that covered most of her body. "Mr. James has driven in circles for nearly an hour."

Adonis allowed an expression of apology. "I was in the haberdashery." He indicated the new scarf. "Took Mr. Turner quite some time to find this in the back. Seems he put away all the winter clothing a few months ago thinking it wouldn't be needed until next winter."

Persephone rolled her eyes. "I can't say I blame him," she replied. "There's not a muff to be found in town," she complained. "Nor a decent fur coat. I certainly didn't expect to have to wear a *coat* to a ball this time of the year," she added in disgust.

Adonis listened to his sister's rant and finally angled his head. "Just what is the date today?" he asked.

Sighing, Persephone stared at her brother for several moments. "You really have lost your faculties, haven't you?" she whispered. When Adonis merely stared back at her, she finally replied, "Fifteenth of June, eighteen-sixteen." She stated the date as if she had already said it several times that day.

Blinking, Adonis was about to argue that he hadn't lost his faculties—the weather was certainly the one to have lost its mind—but he thought better of it. There was no arguing with an older sister, after all.

CHAPTER 1
A VISIT TO THE MUSEUM

June 17, 1816

Lydia regarded the south side of the British Museum, rather surprised to find there wasn't already a line of people in queue for the Monday morning's ten o'clock opening. Montagu House, the building purchased by the Board of Trustees of the museum to house its collections, featured a series of steps leading up to a portico and a set of double doors.

"On a lovely day such as this, the museum is never very crowded, my lady."

Turning to find the driver of her coach-and-four standing at the curb, Lydia nodded. The clear blue sky was dotted with white puffy clouds. The air actually held a hint of warmth, unlike the other spring days that had come before. With no rain in sight—a rare occurrence this particular year—most Londoners who weren't laboring at their jobs would be spending the beautiful day out-of-doors. "Then I shall have the place all to myself," Lydia responded with a grin.

She headed through the museum's front doors, nodding to the driver when he hurried up to open the door for her. "Good day, sir. I shall see you in three hours," she said, allowing her eyes to adjust to the dim interior before making her way into the lobby.

Although she hadn't decided on a particular reason for visiting the museum on this day, Lydia found she had free time to do whatever she pleased. A widow for—had it already been a year?—she paid visits to a lending library as well as *The Temple of the Muses* to acquire the books she read in the late afternoons, she occasionally hosted others in her home for morning tea, she had a private box at the Royal Theatre, and she attended the few evening events for which she received invitations.

Married to a titled man—her husband had been a viscount—Lydia had herself grown up in a family of aristocrats and had always been a lady. As the daughter of the *ton*, she enjoyed some freedoms other widows might not. As the widow of an officer, she collected a meager pension on top of the small fortune she had inherited upon his death.

The news of Viscount Jasper Barrymore's death hadn't been unexpected. Every day during the Peninsular Wars, Londoners received reports from the Continent of British soldiers having died in battle, and if not in battle, then because they perished in the cold or from some horrible wound or disease.

She supposed she should have been surprised at how long her husband managed to survive given his penchant for leading his men from the back of a Friesian. An easy target for a bullet, she was sure, although there was a thought that Jasper had died by the thrust of a bayonet through his midsection. At least, that's what someone from the War Office had suggested. The clerk claimed they didn't know for sure. She never saw his body prior to the graveside service that had him buried in his family's small plot in Kent.

Given his real occupation as a spy, she couldn't even be sure of anything she'd been told.

Lydia Grandby Barrymore was, by all accounts, living the life of an independent woman, although a lonely one these days. A brief *affaire* with one of Jasper's colleagues had ended when he announced he was to be married in a month to a much younger debutante—by necessity, he had assured her.

No doubt because he needed her dowry. That had been just three weeks ago.

Not particularly saddened at the loss of the occasional lover, Lydia merely continued life on the fringes of the *ton*. She didn't employ a companion or force her lady's maid to accompany her on these frequent sojourns from her townhouse in Bruton Street.

If she had any hope of returning to her own occupation once her mourning period was over, she needed to keep her instincts sharp. Hone her skills at observation and listening. And above all, remain as unnoticeable as possible.

Widow's weeds certainly helped in that regard, she considered as she glanced down at her dull black bombazine gown and pelisse. Then she did a visual sweep of the lobby, looking for clues as to what might have changed since her last visit. A rectangular space on one wall, slightly outlined by a darkening of the wallpaper, suggested a painting had been recently removed. The brighter circle in the marble floor told her a display stand had recently been positioned there. Given the high traffic in this part of the museum, it had probably been moved to prevent an artifact from taking a tumble should a patron accidentally brush against it.

She thought of climbing to the upper floor to see the displays of fossils, minerals, and seashells, but decided instead to start in the Gallery. Townley's collection of statues, as well as other Greek, Roman, and Egyptian antiquities, were located there.

The thought of viewing artwork created more than a millennia ago excited Lydia. That someone had the skills to cut and carve marble into such detailed works of art meant the ancestors of humanity weren't the barbaric creatures she had been warned of whilst still in the schoolroom in Merriweather Manor.

For every Spartan, there had been an Athenian, after all.

Viewing statues of mostly naked men would have been nearly impossible if there were too many others with her in the Gallery. On a day such as this, she had the room to herself.

She didn't exactly *study* the statues, but surreptitiously surveyed them as she slowly walked around each one. She found them intriguing. Men nowadays weren't so very different from those of two- or three-thousand years ago, she decided, although she only had experience with the two from current times. Perhaps the Greeks were more beautiful. Youthful, mayhap. Or perhaps they only depicted younger subjects because it was difficult to carve wrinkles into marble.

The reclining man before her was definitely youthful, his body barely muscled, his face relaxed as if he were sleeping. She could almost feel his soft breaths as he lay there, one arm raised above his head and angled so its hand was atop his curly hair whilst the other was bent with its hand resting beneath his chin. He wasn't entirely naked but wore a cape tossed over one shoulder, and the folds of a skirt were strewn about his mid-section. His feet sported sandals with leather ties wrapped about his thick ankles.

Awareness of another's presence in the gallery had the hairs on the back of her neck reacting.

The sensation of a soft breath wafted over her shoulder again, this time bearing the slightest hint of sandalwood and spice cologne. Stiffening where she stood, Lydia realized someone was standing directly behind and to her left. A man, no doubt, given the scent of his cologne. She was about to put voice to a complaint, but he put voice to a most audacious claim before she had a chance.

"I've been told I look exactly like him," the male voice whispered, almost in her ear.

Lydia carefully stepped to the right and turned slightly, amazed to see that, yes, the intruder did indeed look exactly like Adonis. Or *Endymion sleeping on Mount Latmos*, if one remembered the label mounted next to the block of marble. He was also impeccably dressed in a superfine navy topcoat, an elaborately embroidered waistcoat in red and gold, and buckskin breeches that, at the moment, left absolutely nothing to the imagination as far as his muscular thighs and the bit of anatomy that was located just above them. A quick glance at his tasseled boots, and Lydia was sure she could see her reflection. One of his gloved hands was pressed onto the top of a cane handle decorated in ornately-patterned silver plate while the other held what appeared to be a sketchpad.

"You do, in fact," she murmured, her gaze darting back and forth between the statue and his living twin. "Are you related, perhaps?" she asked with an arched eyebrow.

"My mother must have thought so. She named me Adonis," he replied with an equally arched eyebrow.

Lydia turned completely to face the man, taking a step back when she realized just how close he had been standing. "Did she now?" she replied, not exactly sure how to respond to such an odd claim.

Now that she could see his entire face—he really did look like the youth depicted in the statue—she realized he was older. At least ten years older than the Adonis carved in the statue. The planes of his face were sharper, perhaps, and a slight scar ruined his otherwise perfect face just below his right cheekbone. If he had ever attended any *ton* events, she couldn't remember having seen him at them. Probably because he would have been surrounded by debutantes hoping to gain a dance—or his hand in marriage.

The man was positively beautiful.

"It's been my downfall, actually. Whoever takes a gentleman seriously when his name is that of history's most beautiful man?"

Not exactly sure how she was supposed to respond to such a rhetorical question, Lydia merely replied with, "Who, indeed?"

His brows furrowed. "You, I hope."

Lydia blinked and then quickly glanced around, wondering if anyone was paying heed to their conversation. If a gossip should spy them speaking to one another as they were, she could only imagine the stories that might be heard in parlors up and down Park Lane. "I'm quite sure we've never been introduced," she whispered hoarsely, and then moved to the next statue. Another one from Greece, which meant the man was naked. *Why did the Greeks depict their heroes naked when the Romans carved them with their clothes on?* she wondered, realizing her cheeks were probably bright red. Of course her attention went directly to the statue's genitals. At least they were on the small side, and not carved in too much detail.

She wondered if the man who claimed his name was Adonis would follow her, hoping on the one hand he would not, and then, on the other, hoping he would.

What's wrong with me? she quickly admonished herself.

He was no doubt a bounder, a rake, perhaps, accosting ladies as they viewed scantily clad statues of beautiful men. But there was something about him that suggested he was a bit lost. Lonely. His manner of speech suggested he was a gentleman. He was certainly dressed as a man of leisure, and yet...

She whirled around, realizing he *had* followed her. He was once again directly in front of her, closer than was proper, close enough that their foreheads would touch should either one of them lean forward very much. The scent of his cologne wafted over her even as his eyes closed. She watched as he inhaled deeply.

"Your perfume is positively intoxicating," he whispered before slowly reopening his eyes.

Once again, Lydia had no idea how to respond to such a comment. No one had ever put voice to such a claim before —at least, not quite like this. The chemist who had created the perfume for her at Floris merely said it was appropriate for a widow of means. *Orange blossom combined with a hint of spice,* he said, never divulging what spice he had added to make the subtle fragrance. At least, she had thought it subtle. Adonis' claim that it was intoxicating had her wondering if she was giving off more spice than she intended.

Lifting her eyes to meet his, Lydia was startled by how he stared at her. "I really don't think it appropriate for you to say such a thing," she stammered, wondering if she should give the chemist a tip when she next paid a visit to Floris.

"Why ever not?" he countered, a look of hurt crossing his face. "I thought honesty was always best..." He suddenly rolled his eyes before allowing a sigh. "You are right, of course. I forget sometimes." His eyes darted to the side and then refocused on her, as if he were trying to decide what to say next.

Lydia blinked again, wondering if perhaps the man was a simpleton. He spoke well, and yet his conversation was wholly inappropriate. A quick look around assured her no one was watching them, at least. His next words had her on edge, though.

"Perhaps you will join me for a chocolate? I should like us to become acquainted. I should like..."

"We've not been properly *introduced*," she reminded him before turning away, managing a slight curtsy as she did so. She hurried off to another statue. At least this one was of a woman, although she nearly rolled her eyes when she realized it was of Venus. *Lely's Venus*, she remembered as she sighed.

Aphrodite.

The naked goddess was depicted crouching, her head turned sharply to her right, which is exactly what Lydia was forced to do when Adonis was suddenly standing to her right. She was stunned to find him gazing first at the statue and then at her, as if he were comparing them.

"You're far prettier than she is," he stated. "Although her hair is quite beautiful."

Lydia turned her attention back to the statue, studying the elaborate top knot and curls the statue displayed. Noting the woman's face, Lydia allowed an audible sigh. "Given the fact that her nose is missing, it's no wonder you might think that," she whispered, leaning away from the strange gentleman as she made the comment.

She couldn't help the thrill she felt at hearing his declaration, though. Her own hair was dressed rather fine, although her black silk hat covered most of the curls her lady's maid had ironed into them that morning.

"Still, her lips are nothing like yours."

Stiffening until she reached her full five-foot, five-inch height, Lydia inhaled sharply and faced the bounder. Her attention immediately went to the scar on his otherwise perfect face. "And yours are about to be bloodied since I have decided it's time to hurl my reticule in your direction. And that scar on your cheek? Put there, no doubt, by the blade of a jealous husband, was it not?"

The look of surprise and then hurt that appeared on the man's face had Lydia immediately regretting her words. He stepped back so suddenly, he nearly tripped, although he was quick to use his cane to steady himself. Giving her a slight bow, he managed to say, "Good day, my lady," before hurrying away.

"I apologize," Lydia hurried to get out before he was out of earshot, sighing when the man paused only a half-step before he continued, a noticeable limp in his gait as he made his way toward the museum's exit.

That was truly awful of me, she thought as she slowly turned her attention back to the statue.

Her eyes widened when she remembered how vengeful Aphrodite could be when the goddess of love thought her wishes had been ignored or otherwise thwarted. "I feel awful about what just happened," she said in a hoarse whisper, her words directed to the statue. "But that man and me? We haven't been properly introduced," she murmured again, hoping the goddess would have mercy on her.

Mercy?

Or did she want a second chance?

The way the man gazed at her, as if he were memorizing every detail of her face, had another thrill shooting through her body. Did he know she had been doing the same thing with him?

Lydia headed to the upper floors, deciding it would be safer to spend her day with the minerals and seashells.

CHAPTER 2
A PROTECTOR ARRIVES

*L*ater that day

The invitation to Lady Morganfield's annual garden party arrived while Lydia was at the museum; the beautifully penned missive written on a bright, white stationery bearing the Morganfield marquessate's crest at the top. Lydia's butler handed it to her as she stepped into her townhouse's vestibule, explaining that a footman had delivered it with the instructions that it be read as soon as possible.

The tulips are finally in bloom, rather later than usual, which accounts for this notice of some urgency, the feminine script explained at the bottom of the invitation. Indeed, the invitation was for the afternoon next and bore no request for regrets.

Obviously the marchioness wanted to take advantage of the sudden good weather to host her party. Another few days, and the party would probably have to be moved indoors due to a rain shower. Or snow. Goodness! If the weather didn't improve—and for a long period of time—then there would be no flowers!

Of course, Lydia would go to the party. Adeline Carlington's garden parties were always fashionable affairs that offered as much enjoyment as they did an opportunity to donate funds to the marchioness' favorite charity. Lady E's 'Finding Work for the Wounded' was her current favorite, although given it was run by Lady Morganfield's daughter, Lady Bostwick, one couldn't be too surprised at the choice. Besides, unlike most of the charities the ladies of the *ton* started in their own names, this one actually seemed to do some good by finding employment for wounded soldiers. *Old fogeys*, they called them. Soldiers who had returned from the Continent with any manner of impairment, but most able to perform some sort of employment if only someone gave them a chance.

Or bribed an employer to hire them, which is what Lydia thought Lady Bostwick might be doing in order to place some of the wounded soldiers that passed through her charity's doors in Oxford Street.

Well, as long as there were funds to make the bribes and pay a tailor to sew a suit of clothes for each candidate, the charity would continue to exist. Garden parties such as Lady Morganfield's were merely a way of raising some of those funds.

Tulips, Lydia thought as she reread the invitation. She angled her head and wondered if any had appeared in the small garden behind her townhouse. Jenkins, her butler, was about to help her out of her pelisse when she waved him off. "I'm just going to check the back garden," she murmured as she made her way out of the vestibule and into the hall.

"The locksmith hasn't yet paid a call," Jenkins countered.

Lydia slowed her steps and then stopped to regard the butler. "The locksmith?"

Jenkins nodded. "The kitchen maid says she had trouble locking the back door when she came in from picking herbs, my lady," he explained.

Waving a hand, Lydia replied, "I shouldn't think there would be any need to worry. Who would attempt to come into the house without first knocking?" she asked, her head shaking with her words.

A thief. A murderer. A rapist. All the possibles were given their due in her thoughts, but it was far better her servants didn't know she was all too aware of just who might come into a house without knocking.

In her former business, she knew all manner of reasons for broken locks.

Lydia continued on her way, stepping through the troublesome door to find that, yes, indeed, a few tulips were blooming. She made her way on the flagstones that meandered through the modest garden, stopping occasionally to admire a rare bloom or to pick one for a bouquet for the hall table. Studying the flags, she frowned when she noticed footprints made by a boot much larger than her own half-boots.

The gardener, she surmised, continuing her survey of the plants. A quick glance at the bit of lawn proved it had been recently trimmed, and the remains of any dead plants from the year prior had been completely removed.

By the time she had walked the entire path, she had barely gathered enough flowers to make a small arrangement for the hall table. This one rare, clear day among a month of cooler temperatures and incessant rain had her wondering if there would be any more spring flowers. *I might have to install a greenhouse*, she thought, her brows furrowing when she glanced at the meager plantings just behind the house. Although the small kitchen garden to the west held the most greenery, probably because it was close to the house and safe from the near-freezing nighttime temperatures, it wouldn't last the summer if the weather continued as it did.

The sound of a horse had her listening for the accompanying answer from another. When it came, she allowed a grin but didn't bother to look toward the mews at the end of the alley.

On her way back into the house, she turned on the top step to survey the entire back yard. Rather small compared to those behind the mansions in Park Lane, this one featured a winding path leading to a gate that opened to the alley. The red and pink clouds to the west portended another brilliant sunset. With any luck, the good weather would hold for another day to accommodate Lady Morganfield's garden party.

With one final glance, Lydia turned and made her way back into the house. Given her arms were filled with flowers, she shut the door behind her with a shove of an elbow, not bothering to ensure the door latched properly.

From where he stood in the alley, barely hidden at the end of the back fence, Adonis Truscott watched Lady Barrymore make her way into her townhouse. He gave a sigh of relief for two reasons. She had made it home safely from the museum despite not having had a companion or a footman to accompany her, and because she hadn't paid witness to his sudden presence in the alley.

Adonis certainly hadn't expected her to appear in her back garden when she did. His only reason for taking the alley route when he followed her from the museum was to track the carriage in which she rode without having to ride directly behind it.

And then his mount had gone and made a sound of protest.

He was sure she heard the neigh, for he watched as her back stiffened and her head jerked a bit to the right, as if she were listening intently. For just the moment, he was sure he would be discovered, and he rather doubted Lydia would be pleased to learn he had followed her. She would probably be furious given her reaction to him at the museum.

I did make a fool of myself, he thought with a frown. But then, he hadn't known what to say, exactly. Hadn't known how to approach her other than attempt to make conversation. It had been so long since he had put voice to words—other than to his batman and his bothersome sister—he wasn't exactly sure what to say to her when he was finally in her presence.

This used to be so much easier, he thought as he continued to stare at the back of her house. Settle in for a long night, the tools of the trade close at hand—opera glasses, pencil and parchment, a flask of scotch and a pasty. Now he couldn't imagine having to spend a night doing reconnaissance. Spying. Not since that last night on the battlefield. The night that seemed as if it would never end.

He shook his head as if to clear it, determined not to allow his memories to get the better of him just then.

Think of her, he nearly whispered out loud. She was a far better subject on which to spend a moment of thought than something that had happened near Brussels a year ago. Indeed, Lydia Barrymore was far more beautiful than his commander had intimated with his final words. Far more feisty. Far more...

More.

Adonis swallowed.

Lady Barrymore wasn't at all as she had been described. In fact, Adonis had spent the past month ensuring he had the right woman. He had only been back on British shores a month more than that, unable to return at the same time as the other two men who remained of his small unit of operatives assigned to an infantry unit.

His prolonged stay in a hospital in Brussels had prevented an earlier return.

Adonis shook his head, knowing he couldn't allow his thoughts to dwell on his recent past. Doing so only meant losing hours of time. Hours of awareness. Hours of life. Then there would be that sickening moment when he suddenly regained his wits. Even thinking of it made him shake his head from side to side, as if to ward off the haunting spirits of his past.

Leading his horse the rest of the way down the alley, he finally struggled to mount the Cleveland Bay. Trusting the horse to get him to his bachelor quarters in Green Street, Adonis considered what he must do next.

CHAPTER 3
PILLOW TALK

*L**ater that night at Fitzsimmons Manor*

"Christ, it's colder than a witch's tit," Matthew Fitzsimmons, Viscount Chamberlain, complained as he allowed his valet to undo the fastenings of his waistcoat. His own fingers were nearly numb from his quick trip to meet the Earl of Torrington at White's.

"Aye, my lord. I've added more coal to the fire, and there are two hot bricks at the end of your bed," Tipton murmured, tugging the garment from his master's chest.

Matthew pulled his shirt from his head himself, hurrying to get his nightshirt on before the cool air in the room could chill him further. "I can do the rest," he said as he waved off his valet.

"Very good, my lord," Tipton replied, giving a bow before he quickly took his leave of the master bedchamber.

The viscount watched as the door shut, sure he had seen the man's breath turn into a white cloud. He gave a thought as to how cold it must be in his wife's bedchamber. Thought of how warm he might become if he could snuggle up next to her. If she were already asleep, it would be cruel to waken her with his cold body—and his colder feet—but he was determined to get warm.

Doffing his breeches, he was about to head to her

bedchamber by way of the dressing room when Caroline appeared. A silk wrapper pulled tight around her body left little to the imagination. The silhouettes of her hardened nipples poked through the thin fabric and had Matthew's body reacting in kind. He might have been in his mid-fifties, but he was still a man, and the sight of Caroline Harrington Fitzsimmons proved it. Her blonde hair, streaked with hints of golden gray, hung in waves around her shoulders, reminding him of how she always looked like his idea of a mythological siren—and how much he desired her.

"Would you mind very much if I joined you in your bed tonight?" she murmured, her manner almost apologetic. "It's terribly chilly in my room."

Matthew's arms were around her in an instant, pulling her hard against the front of his body. "Bless you, my sweeting," he whispered, his lips taking purchase on her temple. "You're always welcome in my bed," he added in a whisper, his lips moving to her lips to kiss the corner of her mouth.

Caroline blinked as she gazed up at her husband. They had been married for years, and yet Matthew had never shown his affection quite like this. "I am?"

Matthew didn't bother to reply, but rather scooped her into his arms and placed her onto his bed, ignoring her yelp of surprise. He followed a moment later after turning down the bedside lamp. "Of course, Caro," he finally said, stretching out alongside her until one of his feet touched the still-warm cloth-covered brick. Lifting himself onto one elbow, he regarded his wife. Her blonde hair, swept out around her head, appeared as it were a golden halo. "My angel," he whispered.

Gazing at him through half-closed eyes, Caroline reached a hand up to the side of his face. "I'd rather be a bit of a devil tonight," she murmured, the word 'devil' only mouthed. "I would certainly welcome the warmth," she added as she arched an elegant eyebrow to emphasize the invitation.

Desire slammed into Matthew in an instant, his manhood already hard from his having paid witness to the evidence of her erect nipples. His lips were on hers just as quickly, sliding and suckling until they locked into place, until his tongue could slip between her teeth and taste the port they had shared after his return from White's. He reveled in the slight moan he heard emanate from the back of her throat, in how her chest rose beneath his. When she broke the kiss and gasped as if needing air, he simply moved his lips down the column of her throat, nibbling as he went. His tongue delved into the hollow of her throat and circled before moving to trace her collarbones.

At the same time, he felt one of her hands capture his and move it to one of her breasts. Cupping it gently through the silk and the lawn of the nightrail beneath her wrapper, he felt the hardened nipple settle between two fingers.

"Caro," he breathed between kisses, his body warming faster than he thought possible. The ribbon of her silk wrapper was untied, and he realized she had pulled it apart. The buttons on the frilly nightrail beneath had already been undone, leaving one of her breasts bare. His mouth covered it before she could beg him to do so, his other hand giving up his hold on her to slip beneath the fine lawn to caress her other breast and belly. "Jesus, Caro, I want you so badly," he whispered between kisses and nips and nibbles.

Her body undulating beneath him, Caro responded with a whispered, "Yes."

It was all the invitation he needed.

Lifting himself over her body, he settled atop her, shoving the fabric of her nightrail beneath her bottom before he pulled his own entirely from his body.

Sliding his hands beneath the globes of her bottom, he impaled her in a single thrust. Matthew allowed a long sigh as he felt her legs wrap around his back and heard her gasp of surprise. "I apologize," he managed between attempts to breathe.

"Don't you dare," she countered, her hips lifting to counter his first thrust.

Matthew swore into her shoulder, fighting the urge to

simply allow his release. When had Caroline ever initiated relations between them? He couldn't remember her ever doing so, although she had never rebuffed his overtures at lovemaking. *I've been a fool,* he thought before he pulled himself almost entirely from her body. He thrilled at the sound of her protest, thrilled at how her splayed hands gripped his buttocks and pulled him back into her body. The invitation was undeniable, her whispered pleas of, "Yes," merely adding fuel to the fire that had him repeating his thrusts in hard, even movements. At one point, he managed to kiss one of her nipples. A few thrusts later, he kissed the other. His release, well beyond his control, gripped him and stopped his movements at the same moment he heard her final, "Yes."

Suspended above her for the time it took for the pleasure to completely register, Matthew gazed at his wife and wondered why they weren't doing this every night. And then oblivion took him under, took him to ecstasy, and left him there to lose his grip on sanity and the here-and-now.

Physically spent, Matthew could do nothing more than collapse upon the soft body of his wife, his head settling into the pillow next to her head. "You minx," he managed to whisper before sleep took him under.

Caroline closed her eyes and managed a grin, her last thoughts of how warm she finally felt just then.

"We shall have to do this more often," she whispered as she lowered her legs from around his body and reveled in the afterglow of lovemaking. *Especially since you still need an heir.*

When Matthew didn't respond, Caroline knew he was sound asleep. Sighing, she plotted how she might have to awaken him in the middle of the night with a plea to warm her again.

What worked once might work again, she reasoned.

CHAPTER 4
A NOCTURNAL VISITATION

ater that night

Lydia awoke with a start, sure something—or someone—had come into her bedchamber. Holding her breath a moment, she allowed her eyes to adjust to the darkness in the room. The scents of sandalwood and spice had her blinking.

Turning her head to the right, she was stunned to make out the silhouette of a man standing next to her bed. She was about to let out a yelp when she instead took a deep breath. *This cannot be happening*, she whispered to herself. "This is just a dream," she reasoned, rather glad to hear her voice in the stillness. Why ever would there be a man in her bedchamber, after all? Her late husband was... well, he was *dead*, and Oliver was about to be married and off on his wedding trip to the Continent.

"That explains it, I suppose. What a relief."

The sound of the hoarse whisper had Lydia sitting up straight in the bed, her sudden inhalation of breath rather loud in the otherwise quiet bedchamber. She pulled the bed linens up to her neck and was about to scream when she realized it might really be just a dream. If so, she would seem rather ridiculous waking the entire household over a figment of her nocturnal imagination. She instead elected to ignore the man and simply stare straight ahead into the darkness.

Had she been dreaming? The wisps of whatever she'd been experiencing just before she woke up danced before her eyes. A man, caressing her face, his lips barely touching hers... a whisper to sleep... the sensation of warmth...

She could remember nothing else. Relaxing a bit and just about to settle herself back into the pillows, she was startled to discover the apparition was still there. The dark shape hadn't disappeared but had instead settled onto the edge of the bed. She knew it because she felt the mattress depress. The unmistakeable sound of boots falling to the floor had her gasping again. "Who is there?"

In the dark, she could make out a shirt being removed before the man returned to his feet. "Who would you like me to be?"

Gone, Lydia almost replied, but thought better of it. This had to be a dream, after all. Why not allow it to play itself out to its conclusion? "Who would *you* like to be?" she whispered in reply, rather liking how breathy the question sounded in the stillness.

Two could play at this game.

"Your protector."

Lydia blinked, disappointed at the simple response. "Oh," she managed before allowing a sigh, not bothering to hide her disappointment. *Well, this is most curious.* She rather hoped the man would say something like, *Your knight in shining armor*, or *Your next lover.*

"Your next lover, perhaps." The words were spoken out loud, although they sounded gentle, almost too quiet in the darkness.

Could the man read her mind?

Well, of course, he could! He was a player in her dream!

A thrill of excitement shot through her body just then. The same kind of thrill she experienced when Oliver arrived and informed her he would be spending the night in her company. A thrill that had her breasts growing heavy, and the space at the top of her thighs throbbing in anticipation.

If only Oliver had been as good a lover as he thought he was, she might have discovered just why her body reacted as it did. Why she was always left feeling as if there should have been more to a lover's caress. More to what happened during intercourse.

"Eventually, at least. I hope," the man added in a whisper.

The thrill ceased.

"Oh?" she whispered, attempting to mask the sense of disappointment she felt at hearing his qualifying comment. Even before she could put voice to a query, she was aware of the linens and quilt being pulled down. The mattress once again depressed, this time to accommodate an entire body. One of his arms reached around her waist, pulling and turning her body so her back was pressed against the front of his. She managed to quell the urge to cry out, instead concentrating on the feel of his muscular forearm beneath her questing hand, the way in which his knees bent behind her own, the way the back of her thighs settled against his... *bare thighs?* They had to be, for her own were barely covered by her nightrail, and she felt no prickly wool through the fabric. Her bottom ended up tucked into his bent body, the evidence of his arousal pressed into the fine lawn covering her backside.

The slight tug at the neckline of her nightrail told her the bow was no longer tied. The fine lawn slid over one shoulder, baring it to the cool air of the bedchamber.

She inhaled softly when she felt the pressure of his firm lips on the top of the exposed shoulder. The kiss, barely there and yet so compelling, left a hint of moisture behind. Aware of his breath on it, she nearly shivered as it cooled the spot.

"Go back to sleep, my sweeting," he murmured.

Lydia blinked. "But I thought I already was," she whispered in protest.

The arm around her waist slowly relaxed, and it was then she realized the hand at the end of it cradled her bare breast. Somehow, the man had managed to open the front of her nightrail. *Or perhaps I did*, she thought with not the least bit of shame, remembering when the tie had come undone.

She closed her eyes and inhaled deeply, the scent of sandalwood once again apparent in the air. *He smells like the man at the museum*, she thought. *Adonis.*

Such a beautiful man, she remembered with a sigh. Despite the scar that marred his cheek and the look of hurt that seemed to haunt his eyes, he was a beautiful man.

I was so rude to him, she remembered. *How could I say such a thing to a man I have never met before?*

Another part of her argued that she had no choice. The man had proved an annoyance. A potential scandal for a widow, even if her mourning period had reached the one-year mark and was, for all intents and purposes, complete.

I'm so tired, she thought with a sigh, allowing her body to settle against the one that held her, deciding she would simply accept the dream and allow it to run its course.

What harm could come from being held by a dream?

The moment she reasoned her nocturnal visitor had to be real, had to be Adonis—in the flesh—she opened her eyes. Struggling to sit up, she was stunned to discover she was by herself in the bed. In fact, in the dim light of morning, she could find no evidence of him—or anyone else—anywhere in her bedchamber.

A combination of disappointment and relief settled over her as she returned her head to her pillow, ignoring the scent of sandalwood that wafted from the pillow next to hers.

She was saved from giving it too much thought when her maid peeked her head around the edge of the bed curtains. Goodness! She hadn't even heard the maid come into the bedchamber!

"Good morning, my lady. Are you ready to dress?"

When the sound of rain didn't make itself apparent, Lydia allowed a smile. "I am," she replied with a happy sigh.

Dreams could be rather satisfying if she just let them happen. She would have to work on making sure the next one wasn't so chaste, though.

CHAPTER 5
ON THE TOPIC OF SPIES

The following morning, June 18, 1816, at the Foreign Office in Whitehall

Matthew Fitzsimmons, Viscount Chamberlain, rubbed his cheek with an ink-stained hand and cursed. Loudly. He might have started the day on a rather happy note—he awoke to find the warm, soft body of his wife nestled against the side of his rather misshapen, overweight body and remembered the quiet lovemaking that had sent him into a deep sleep just before dawn—nothing good had come of his first few hours at Whitehall. He had a brief thought of simply leaving the Foreign Office and heading for home with the thought of bedding his wife again. *No wonder Grandby is always in such a good mood,* he thought as he remembered how positively joyous Milton Grandby, The Earl of Torrington, had been at White's the night before.

Chamberlain's clerk, Andrew Higgins, trained to at least appear on the threshold of his open door whenever the viscount called out, was on his way to do so when his attention was diverted to the man who appeared at his own office door.

"How do, Higgins?" Adonis Truscott said as he gave the clerk a nod.

Higgins blinked, obviously stunned. He blinked again. "You're not dead," he whispered in response.

It was Adonis' turn to blink. "No. At least, I don't think I am," he replied, his brows furrowing until a crease appeared between them. His eyes suddenly widened. It had been some time since he had been in contact with the Foreign Office. His last orders were to simply return to London and report when his leg was healed enough to allow him to walk. Although he still required a cane on occasion, he could walk, albeit with a limp. "Was I supposed to be? For if I was, I didn't receive the order..." He stopped speaking, realizing it was rather unlikely he'd be ordered to die, and putting voice to the possibility seemed rather ridiculous just then.

It would, in fact, only add to the rumors that he was insane.

The clerk shook his head while waving his hands in front of him. "No, no, it's nothing like that. It's just... we didn't receive word of you after Ligny," he said as he hurried to lead Adonis to the viscount's office. "Or, at least, *I* didn't." He dared a glance in the direction of the director's door, realizing Lord Chamberlain probably knew all along that Adonis Truscott was alive and in one piece. "Chamberlain will be relieved to see you, I'm sure," he added in a huff.

Adonis nodded, realizing just then that Higgins hadn't been informed of his survival. He was quite sure Lord Chamberlain knew, for the orders he had received whilst he was still in a Brussels hospital were quite clear.

Take the time you need to recover. When you can walk again, pay a call.

The paper had been folded into a neat square and secured with Chamberlain's seal.

At least, it might have been secure when it left Chamberlain's office.

There was evidence the note had been opened more than once on its way to Brussels. Given its lack of an apparent code or secret message embedded therein, it reached him in relatively good condition.

At the memory of the day he had received the missive, Adonis was tempted to simply halt his steps and give the memory its due. Spend a few minutes remembering everything about where he was at the time—a hospital in war-torn Brussels filled with wounded and dying soldiers.

Everything he heard—voices speaking medical phrases in French and German.

Everything he smelled—the iron tang of blood and the sickening scent of putrefaction.

Everything he touched...

He stopped in place and jerked back to the here and now when he heard the viscount bellow his clerk's name again.

"Perhaps I'll just wait until he's finished with you," Adonis suggested, one finger of the hand that held a sketchpad lifted to point toward the door of the man who was in charge of planning and strategic operations for the Foreign Office.

Higgins shook his head. "Please, sir, if you would? He's been... *perturbed* about something all morning. I'm sure your appearance will change his poor nature."

Rolling his eyes, Adonis murmured, "You owe me," before dutifully stepping into Matthew Fitzsimmons' office. Higgins did so a moment later, standing at attention until the viscount finally lifted his head.

And did a double-take.

"About damn time you made an appearance," Chamberlain stated as he pushed back his chair and stood up. The words might have sounded harsh, but the viscount displayed a huge grin as he said them.

Adonis nodded. "Reporting as ordered, my lord," he replied, leaning heavily on his silver-topped cane. He moved his sketchpad so it rested under his left arm.

The viscount approached and held out his right hand. "Better late than never, of course," he countered, shaking Adonis' hand as he clapped his other hand against his visitor's shoulder. His attention went to Higgins, who hovered in the doorway. "Shut the door, and don't let anyone in."

"Of course, my lord," Higgins said as he backed out of the office and pulled the door closed behind him until the latch clicked.

Adonis was sure he heard the man's sigh of relief at not having to spend another moment in Matthew Fitzsimmons' presence. Something had the viscount upset, or at least it had before Adonis appeared.

The viscount indicated the chair in front of his desk as he moved to take his own. "I'm sure Higgins must have thought he saw a ghost when he caught sight of you," he murmured in amusement.

Adonis angled his head to one side. "Something like that," he replied. "But surely *you're* not surprised I'm still alive."

Chamberlain set aside the letter he had been writing and regarded his operative. "Of course not. I've just been careful in whom I've let know about you." He paused a moment. "The king knows, of course, since you're scheduled to be knighted tomorrow morning. If you didn't show up of your own accord today, I was afraid I was going to have to hire a Bow Street Runner to find you. Would have made my office look mighty incompetent if one of my men didn't appear for the ceremony..."

Adonis blinked. "*Knighted?*" he repeated. "Tomorrow? Why wasn't I informed?" Well, Jasper Barrymore had intimated he would earn a knighthood for what he had done that day near Brussels. But how did the news get to the Foreign Office? His commander and fellow spy had died on the battlefield, and as far as Adonis knew, no one had been tasked with recording any last wishes.

Well, there had been the man's one last directive, although it had nothing to do with service to King and country.

"Why?" he asked as he reached down for the sketchpad and opened it to reveal one particular drawing.

Chamberlain grinned. "I don't think I need to spell it out for you," he replied. "For one thing, you and two others of mine managed to survive. And, as for the other, I think the fact that Napoleon was defeated thanks to your false communiques with his agents is quite enough, *Sir Donald*," he added, saying the name with more emphasis than it deserved.

Sir Donald. Well, it did sound better than 'Sir Adonis', he supposed, knowing the viscount was well aware of his real name. The name his mother had bestowed on him when he was still a child.

His father would never have approved, but at that point, Franklin Truscott was dead and buried in the family plot in Kent.

The comment that he and two others had survived meant at least one of the other two men had been able to deliver their messages to Wellington—he knew he had failed that fateful day. He was fairly certain Oliver Preston hadn't made it to the rendezvous point, either. That just left Alistair Comber. The second son of an earl, Alistair had a commission and should have acted as an officer in the British Army, but he had instead gone undercover for Chamberlain to determine who might be acting as a double agent—the Foreign Office was quite sure one among them was acting for the French, and might still be doing so.

Adonis tore the drawing from the sketchpad and held it out. "I brought this as a means of documenting what happened that day." He didn't add that it was the last decent drawing he'd been able to complete. All the others in his sketchpad looked as if they'd been done by amateurs—by children—as if his mind's eye could no longer form complete images for him to use as models, When his subject was right in front of him, he could still do a decent rendering, though, so he knew his skills as an artist were still intact.

Frowning, Chamberlain took the thick parchment from Adonis and stared at it for several seconds. Extremely detailed and nearly life-like in its rendering of Jasper Barrymore, the drawing depicted the moment when the commander was stabbed by a French soldier. All around him, the chaos of battle was drawn with the same attention to detail, as if Adonis had memorized everything else that had happened in the nightmarish scene. "Jesus, Truscott," the viscount murmured as he gave the drawing another look. "May I... keep this? I know there has been some question as to how Barrymore died," he said, his attention still on the drawing. He brought it closer to his face and reached for a pair of spectacles to more closely examine one particular part of the drawing.

"Of course. I have seen quite enough of it." *Every day and every night*, Adonis thought sadly.

Chamberlain set the drawing off to his right and turned his attention back to Adonis. "Leg still giving you fits?" he asked, nodding to the cane Adonis still held in place with one gloved hand.

Shrugging, Adonis considered how to respond. "The cold... when it warms up, it will be fine, I'm sure," he struggled to get out.

"My knees know when it's cold before I do," Chamberlain claimed. "Which is pretty much all the time these days."

Well, except for last night. His knees hadn't protested one iota when he was making love to his wife. Of course, by then, his entire body had been an inferno, generating a good deal of heat in response to Caro's soft cries and incessant pleas of 'yes'.

God, how he loved that word!

"Now, about your next assignment—"

"I cannot leave London," Adonis interrupted with a sudden shake of his head.

The viscount straightened in his chair, rather stunned at his operative's words. "Why ever not?"

Adonis took a breath and let it out slowly. "I... I made a promise, you see, and I cannot keep that promise if I'm not in London."

Lord Chamberlain stared at Adonis for several seconds

before he frowned. "To whom did you make this... promise?" he asked.

Dipping his head, Adonis took a moment before he finally replied. "Commander Barrymore." He gave his head a quick shake. "Viscount Barrymore." He shook his head again. "Jasper."

The viscount settled back into his chair and lifted his steepled fingers to his chin. "You were with him. When he died," he said, not making the statement a question. He gave a quick glance at the drawing, realizing Adonis had been an eye witness to the carnage of that battle. Chamberlain's gaze suggested he was deep in thought, but only for a moment. Jasper Barrymore had been the fourth in that group of operatives, but his message was far different than the one that had been carried by the other three. He had obviously managed to deliver his, even though it ultimately led to his death. Matthew wondered for a moment if the viscount knew he would lose his life at the crossroads near Ligny. The entire campaign had been a disaster until Waterloo.

Adonis nodded. "And for several hours before that," he agreed. "I'm afraid our small band of operatives didn't exactly complete our assignment..." Commander Barrymore—Viscount Barrymore when he wasn't off leading an infantry unit on the Continent—should have survived and been escorted to a waiting ship on the coast.

"Actually, Comber succeeded," Chamberlain stated, realizing just then that Adonis had spent the past year thinking the mission had failed. "You did what you could, and it turned out to be enough. The world is rid of Napoleon, and the war is over. As for your next assignment—"

"I cannot leave London," Adonis repeated, the words sounding as if he hadn't already said them only a moment ago.

"Then you're the perfect candidate for this assignment, Sir Donald," Chamberlain stated as he leaned forward.

Adonis swallowed and regarded the viscount for a moment, rather stunned by the words. The Foreign Office assignments were almost always in another country, unless there was the rare operation that required agents from both the Home Office and the Foreign Office to work together. Those assignments generally involved infiltrating smuggling rings. "Very good, my lord," he finally replied before settling in to hear the particulars of his new orders.

Determined not to retreat into his head, Adonis listened intently and nodded his understanding as Matthew Fitzsimmons detailed the instructions for his next assignment. The edict to ferret out a possible traitor in their midst was perfectly reasonable, especially given Adonis hadn't been in the country for very long and would be unexpected by the free-lance operative. The other order had him a bit surprised. He wondered the entire time if Jasper Barrymore had somehow sent word back to Lord Chamberlain about a certain person's importance before his death on the battlefield. Then Adonis assured the viscount he would get started right away, and he took his leave of Whitehall.

Adonis managed to make it back to his rooms in Green Street before the memories of his last night with Jasper Barrymore had him lost in thought. The memories that included the promise he had made.

When he finally emerged from his reverie nearly an hour later, he thought it rather interesting that the promise he had made to his commander and fellow spy was now part of his next mission as a spy for the Foreign Office.

How did Chamberlain find out?

The question had him thinking hard, but only for a moment. He had a fellow operative to visit, and after that, a social engagement to attend.

CHAPTER 6
TWO COLLEAGUES RENEW
AN ACQUAINTANCE

ater that morning
Oliver Preston regarded his visitor with an arched eyebrow. If he was surprised at seeing Adonis Truscott, he didn't show it, but then the man had always been known for his dour demeanor. He was also dangerous when he needed to be. In his line of work, it was a requirement.

"Truscott. I wondered when you might pay a call," Oliver remarked as he pushed his chair away from his desk. He stood up and made his way to where his visitor stood leaning on a cane, his right hand outstretched.

"My apologies for not having done so when I first returned to London," Adonis said as he shook his colleague's hand. *Former colleague*, he amended to himself. Knowing what he did now, Adonis never would have voluntarily spent time in the man's company. Although Oliver was a handsome man, gently bred women probably found him a bit too rugged looking for their tastes. A bit too Whitechapel. A bit too dark and dangerous.

Adonis' reason would have been far more important. Far more critical to King and country.

"Heard you had some trouble near Brussels," Oliver said

as he waved Adonis to a set of chairs in front of the study's fireplace.

Given the modest size of Oliver Preston's bachelor quarters in Golden Square, Adonis was impressed by the size of the study. That is, until he remembered it was probably only one of two or three rooms. "A bit, yes," Adonis replied. "Shame about Barrymore, though," he added, watching Oliver to see how the man might react to hearing their mutual colleague's name.

"Tragic, is more like it," Oliver replied as he took a seat in a deep upholstered chair. Its worn fabric and the fact that the chair Adonis was about to sit in wasn't a match suggested it was a cast-off—probably from the parlor of some poor widow Oliver had laid claim to. And laid. "I've made attempts to console his widow, of course, but now that I'll be leg-shackled by this time next week..." He allowed the sentence to trail off, apparently expecting well wishes from his visitor. "Got myself a debutante with a decent dowry. She's not much to look at, but she'll do," he commented, as if he had found his future bride at the market whilst shopping for that night's meat course.

Adonis couldn't help the flash of anger he felt at hearing Oliver's comment about Jasper Barrymore's widow. Lady Barrymore knew what her husband did for King and country. She knew because she had worked in the Foreign Office, her skills at solving puzzles and decoding missives better than most of the clerks who worked for Chamberlain. As for if she had any feelings for the man she had married—most assumed theirs was a marriage of convenience—Adonis didn't yet know. He did know Jasper held her in high regard, his last words rather clear on the matter.

His last words...

Adonis shook his head, realizing if he gave them too much consideration at that moment, he would later come to find Oliver waving a hand in front of his face and asking if he was mad.

"Then, I suppose best wishes are called for," Adonis remarked in genuine surprise. "I must say, I wouldn't have expected you to be caught in the parson's trap."

Oliver shrugged. "It's time is all. But enough about me. Where have *you* been?"

Adonis regarded his host and considered what to admit as to his whereabouts for the last year. "I was in a hospital in Brussels until recently," he replied with a shrug. "Nearly lost my leg—a horse stepped on it, you see, and one doctor wanted to saw it off. But a physician there insisted I be his test case. He was sure he could save it with some kind of special surgery. Who was I to argue?" he added with a shrug. He couldn't have if he wanted to—he'd been in a coma at the time, a blessed period that provided relief from pain even though his nightmares were probably worse.

Oliver grimaced and actually paled. "Jesus," he murmured. "Can't say I wished I were there."

His visitor arched an eyebrow. "Where were *you?*" he asked, feigning ignorance. Adonis knew Oliver was somewhere in the Netherlands.

"My assignment had me in Antwerp. Nothing exciting, mind you," Oliver said with a shrug. "Just had to avoid some frogs intent on blowing up the Dutch countryside with their damned cannons. And then, when I could no longer avoid them, I had to join them on one of their excursions." He rolled his eyes, although his manner was almost one of humor.

Adonis had a hard time keeping a passive expression on his face. He knew something of those cannons. Something of what they were capable. He swallowed hard in attempt to keep his attention on the here and now. If he thought too much about that day north of Antwerp ...

He jerked his head up when he realized Oliver was waving a hand in front of his face. *Damn! I've gone and done it again.*

"Doesn't exactly bring back good memories for me,

either," Oliver said. "Especially watching one of those wind-mills come tumbling down. Feats of engineering those are, although so many of them look as if they're ready for retire-ment. Well, that one was certainly retired when the cannon ball hit it, I'll tell you."

Adonis blinked. And blinked again. He forced himself to breathe. Forced himself to remain as calm as possible, for if he did not, Oliver Preston would end up with a cane impaling his throat. "I was at Ligny when this happened," he said quietly, indicating his leg.

Oliver shifted in his chair. "Oh? I heard that's where Barrymore died. Bayonet or some such?"

His visitor nodded. "I heard the same," he agreed, deciding not to admit he was under the man's command at the time. That he was so close, he saw what happened. That he ended up sitting next to the wounded commander for hours and hours. "Did you... complete your assignment? Are you still...?"

"Working for Chamberlain?" Oliver finished for him. "Yes, but not very much these days, although since the war has been over, there really hasn't been much work for those of us who are independents, so to speak. Hence, the need for a wife."

Allowing a look of feigned surprise, Adonis angled his head. "You don't think you'll... miss it?"

Oliver shook his head. "Nah. I just have one little assign-ment to complete, and then I can be off on my wedding trip. Thinking of a jaunt to the Continent."

Stiffening, Adonis was curious about what 'little assign-ment' the man could mean. Chamberlain had been quite clear with his order. Oliver Preston was finished as far as the Foreign Office was concerned, so whatever bit of espionage Oliver was involved in was for another party. Another employer.

Another country.

"I find myself with some time on my hands since I'm

considered an old fogey now." He lifted the cane as a reminder about his noticeable limp. "Anything I can help with?" he offered.

His host gave a one-shouldered shrug. "Only if you knew Barrymore well enough to figure out where he might have kept a ring," he replied and then quickly shook his head. "Forget I said anything—"

"If he was wearing it on the battlefield, it would have been nicked by one of the damned urchins who cleaned out all the dead bodies of their valuables," Adonis interrupted. "They even tried to get my signet, and I was still alive, the little bastards," he complained, holding up his right hand to display a square onyx embedded in a gold band.

Oliver frowned, his brows furrowed so a fold of skin developed between them. "Damn," he murmured, a look of worry crossing his face. He suddenly brightened. "Well, that may be the end of that assignment then," he commented. "Have you the time for a drink? I have some scotch, although it's not particularly good," he said as he motioned toward a sideboard.

"I thank you for the offer," Adonis replied, "But I have a garden party to attend. Perhaps another time? When you're a married man?" he teased with an arched eyebrow.

Rolling his eyes again, Oliver gave a guffaw and straightened his waistcoat. "Perhaps when *you're* a married man," he countered with an arched brow. Then he laughed out loud when Adonis' look of astonishment appeared, as if his fellow operative had never given a thought to becoming leg-shackled. "Now you know exactly how I *really* feel about the matter," he whispered hoarsely.

Oliver saw Adonis to the door of the study and shook his hand again. "I'm glad you made it, Truscott. You're one of the good ones," he remarked with a sigh.

Adonis nodded and took his leave of Oliver Preston's apartments, quite sure Lord Chamberlain was correct in his assessment of Oliver Preston. The man had been a double-agent. Was *still* an agent for another country. A traitor to King and country.

And if he had been among those that destroyed a particular windmill north of Antwerp with a cannon ball, then he was a murderer as well.

CHAPTER 7
A GARDEN PARTY BEGETS
AN INTRODUCTION

ater that day
  A feeling of unease had Lydia pausing at the entrance to Carlington House. She knew she wasn't arriving too early for the marchioness' garden party, but the day's weather, which had begun rather sunny and clear, was suddenly turning. The slight breeze evident when she left her townhouse and climbed into her town coach felt chilly.

Would winter ever give up its claim over England?

Perhaps she shouldn't have spent the day before indoors. Had she not gone to the British Museum, she wouldn't have experienced the unfortunate incident with the man who claimed his name was Adonis. She might have spent the day riding in the park, or taking a stroll in Kensington Gardens, or sitting under the maple trees in Berkeley Square enjoying an ice or a lemonade from Gunter's Tea Shop. Instead, she had communed with a collection of marble statues thousands of years old and breathed in the musty air given off by ancient artifacts.

No wonder she'd had such odd dreams the night before!

But she had also breathed in the scent of a rather enticing cologne.

The sandalwood and spice cologne of Adonis. She could almost smell the scent this very moment. The pillow next to hers seemed to have given off the scent, making her wonder if perhaps a pillow covering from her late husband's bed linens might have been mixed up with hers when the household maid had last changed the sheets. Although, when Lydia gave it some more thought, she couldn't remember Jasper having worn a similar scent. What she could remember of him was a scent closer to that of the laundry soap used to wash his shirts and cravats. Citrus—lemon, mostly—with just a hint of spice.

Lydia blinked. How odd that she thought of Jasper just then. She conjured an image of him in her mind's eye, a bit concerned when she didn't feel the usual sadness. Today's venture would be her first garden party since word of her husband's death reached her. Her mourning period was over. It was time to consider the future. Time to begin living it.

Probably time to return to work as well. Boredom would consume her if she didn't have something intriguing to occupy her time.

She allowed a sigh as she was about to lift the lion-head knocker on the front door of Carlington House. The door opened before she could do so, revealing Alfred, a rather staid butler who was said to be one of the most reserved butlers in all of Park Lane.

"Lady Barrymore for Lady Morganfield's garden party," she murmured as she stepped into the vestibule.

"Do you wish to keep your pelisse, my lady?" he asked with an arched brow. "I hear the weather is turning."

The sense of disappointment Lydia felt just then had her smile faltering. She knew how important this garden party was to Lady Morganfield. Adeline counted on it as a means to raise monies for her charities. If the day grew cold, people would make an abbreviated visit and claim their presence was expected elsewhere. "If I need it, I'll simply return here for it," she replied with a nod, shedding the pelisse with almost no help from the butler.

This event represented the first opportunity she had in

nearly twelve months to wear a gown other than widow's weeds, and she was determined to allow the gown to be seen.

The soft apricot muslin, sprigged with green leaves and tiny blossoms in a darker peach, was probably a better choice for a younger matron than she, but she dearly loved how her modiste had done the elaborate folded gathers at the tops of the sleeves and how she had repeated the pattern in the neckline's edge. Lydia's short gloves, made of silk and dyed to match, were the same shade as the nearly flat hat she wore at a rakish angle over one ear. A dark green parasol hung from a leather strap at her wrist. Her maid had claimed she looked rather smart just before Lydia took her leave of her bedchamber. Although she rarely took Rachel's comments too seriously, she believed her lady's maid today.

Despite having experienced the oddest dreams the night before—she was quite sure one included Adonis and her in a compromising position—she felt happier this day than she had in weeks. The gown she wore merely emphasized her mood.

"Lady Barrymore, so glad you could join us," Adeline Carlington, Marchioness of Morganfield, said with a brilliant smile when Lydia emerged from the French doors at the back of the house. A small group of ladies were assembled near a table set up with champagne flutes and trays of biscuits and tiny sandwiches.

"Oh, call me Lydia, please. Thank you for the invitation. Word of your tulips had me visiting my own gardens to discover if mine might have bloomed, as well," she replied as she curtsied.

"And? Have they?" Adeline countered, one dark eyebrow arched in query. The Italian daughter of a count always looked far more exotic than any English miss ever could.

"A few, along with some very late daffodils. I cannot believe how uncooperative the weather has been for flowers this year."

"No one can," Adeline agreed, hooking her arm into Lydia's so that she could lead her newest guest to the group of ladies already assembled near the refreshment table on the back lawn. "Lady Devonville claims her husband knows a man who can explain why we're not having a spring—something to do with volcanos—but I have yet to learn the particulars."

The comment had Lydia's eyebrows arching up.

Volcanos?

She frowned in concentration, wondering where a volcano might have erupted that would cause the inclement weather they were experiencing in England. She shook her head when she realized the marchioness had paused before a group of women.

Lydia immediately recognized everyone there. Adele Slater Worthington, sister to William Slater, Marquess of Devonfield, and a widow herself, hurried to join her. "So glad you have finally put away the widow's weeds," she said in a quiet voice.

Lydia nodded and then angled her head. "I hear best wishes are in order for you. Is it true you've become a countess?" she asked in a voice she didn't intend to be overheard by the others. "To my cousin?"

Adele nodded. "Indeed. Grandby proposed in March, and we married in April. I still have to pinch myself in the mornings when I wake up." She paused a moment and then arched an elegant eyebrow. "At least, I do on the mornings when Grandby hasn't done it first," she added with a grin.

Giggling, Lydia felt her cheeks grow warm at the implication of the countess' words. At least Adele had married for affection this time. No one knew if she had done so with her first husband, Samuel Worthington. The man had been a pioneer in steam ship design and production, capitalizing on the invention at the perfect time to make a fortune. Taking a marquess' daughter as a wife was considered a coup for the man.

Worthington enjoyed squiring Adele to *ton* events and spending his money on a large mansion in Park Lane as well as on the accoutrements to decorate it. Before he could fully enjoy the fruits of his labors or sire an heir, though, he had died unexpectedly.

Adele had barely ceased wearing widow's weeds when James Weston, a cousin of the renowned tailor to the *ton*, started paying calls. A whirlwind courtship followed, and the two were only weeks from their wedding when Adele learned the true reason Weston wished to wed her.

He needed her fortune to cover his excessive gambling debts.

Adele called off the wedding, well aware of how it would make her look in Society's eyes. She found she didn't care—that she didn't *need* to care what might happen as a result of her spurning the rogue.

Her brother, William Slater, Marquess of Devonville, was rather surprised to learn she had quit the betrothal, but assured her he would support her decision. It's not as if she needed his wealth to help her situation. She had her own fortune thanks to her first husband, and that fortune meant she had a bit of leeway when it came to censure.

A good deal of leeway, actually.

Thinking she would simply remain a widow and enjoy life as an independent woman, Adele was quite surprised when someone else had plans for her.

Most of the *ton* wondered if Milton Grandby, Earl of Torrington, would ever take a wife—he was well into his forties—and most thought that when he did, it would be to a woman much younger than he. Perhaps even to one of the one-and-twenty daughters of the aristocracy for whom he had taken on the honor—and responsibility—of godfatherhood.

He surprised them on both accounts by courting Adele, a woman only a few years younger than him. He stood by her side as she hosted her annual *musicale*, and he escorted her to any number of *ton* events during the early months of the year. By April, they were married, although no one could claim to have paid witness to the vows. Given his earldom was in Northumberland, most thought Grandby had simply whisked her off to Gretna Green and eloped and then taken her on a wedding trip to the seat of his earldom.

Lydia thought it a rather romantic story, one she never thought possible for herself. How often could a lady of the *ton* find love the second time around?

When their hostess was called away by another guest, Lydia allowed Adele to lead her to the other group of women in attendance. Clarinda Fitzwilliam, Countess of Norwick, appeared rather elegant in a long-sleeved teal gown of superfine. Elizabeth Carlington Bennett-Jones, Viscountess Bostwick and daughter of Adeline, bore the unmistakeable posture of a woman growing round with child. Patience Comber, Countess of Aimsley, older than all of them, was the proud mother of two grown sons—one of whom Lydia knew had reported to Chamberlain during part of his service—and a daughter who was attending finishing school in Switzerland. And Caroline Fitzsimmons, Viscountess Chamberlain, displayed a glow that Lydia knew quite well—that of a woman who had been thoroughly tumbled and who had loved every minute of it.

Bravo, Lord Chamberlain, she thought, reminded that she really needed to pay a call on the viscount. *Later today*, she decided.

The women exchanged pleasantries until a chilly wind had several deciding to move their conversation indoors. Lydia would have followed, but Adele continued to hold onto her arm.

"I wonder if you might be amenable to an introduction?" Adele murmured as they moved to the other end of the refreshment table. "I shouldn't want you thinking I am attempting to play matchmaker, because I am not, but a gentleman has requested a formal introduction to you, and I find I'm a bit curious as to his intentions."

Lydia angled her head, rather surprised by the countess' words. What gentleman could have asked for an introduction? "Of course, I don't mind," she said with a shrug, rather amused at Adele's claim she wasn't playing matchmaker. A thrill of excitement shot through her at the thought that a gentleman had asked about her, though. A counter thought that he might be an opportunist simply after her fortune dampened the thrill. "Who is it?"

Adele brought them past a hedgerow and into part of the gardens somewhat hidden from the hardy guests who still milled about the freshly cut lawn. "He's an acquaintance of Torrington's," she remarked, nodding her head to indicate the secluded area in which several tulips were in bloom.

There, a man of about thirty leaned heavily on a silver-topped cane, his attention on a red tulip he held between a thumb and forefinger. At the sight of Lady Torrington and Lady Barrymore, he quickly straightened.

Adele took the opportunity to make the introductions. "Lady Barrymore, I'd like you to meet Sir Donald Truscott. He's actually scheduled to be knighted tomorrow morning—"

"It's an honor to make your acquaintance, my lady," the man interrupted, seemingly oblivious to Adele's attempt at a complete introduction, his gloved hand reaching for Lydia's before she could even offer it.

Lydia could barely form the words, "And yours," for she quickly realized that the knight who stood before her was the man who claimed his name was Adonis.

The man who had been in the museum just the day before.

The man she had offended with her verbal guess as to how he had gained the scar on his otherwise perfect right cheek.

Sir Donald.

Adonis.

Well, it made sense in a way, she supposed.

Her hand was suddenly in his, and despite the silk fabric of her gloves and the kid leather of his, she had a moment when she was quite sure her skin made contact with his, as if they had actually touched one another. A pleasant shiver of shock raced up her arm, nearly to her elbow.

His lips pressed the knuckles of her gloved hand before he straightened and said, "I forgive you, of course. I fear I was too fast in removing myself from your presence yesterday to put voice to my... forgiveness." This last was said after a moment where he seemed to struggle to find the appropriate word. Indeed, he seemed to have difficulty keeping eye contact, as if he were embarrassed—or completely unsure of himself.

Lydia blinked, stunned at the knight's words and well aware of how Adele must have wondered at them, and at the man's odd behavior. *Faith! What must the countess think?*

Lydia finally reclaimed her hand from the knight's gentle grip, noting the fine leather of his black kid glove. She glanced over at Adele and gave a slight shrug, hoping the countess would find a reason to leave them alone, and then hoped she would not.

What more could she say to the gentleman?

At least she now knew he was a gentleman and not some rogue intent on taking advantage of a woman who wasn't in the company of a maid or a chaperone.

The countess' attention was on someone to her left, though, and she gave a quick curtsy. "Pardon me for a moment. Lady Morganfield is summoning me," she said, managing to give Lydia a look that suggested she would still be nearby should her presence be required.

Lydia nodded and lowered her eyes before turning her attention to the knight. "My words of yesterday were unpardonable. I am not usually so rude, I assure you," she murmured, noting how the man still seemed to have difficulty making eye contact. "Not ever, in fact."

"You are pardoned, my lady," Sir Donald replied with a nod. "I realize now I should have first requested an introduction. Accosting you in the museum as I did was... inappropriate. I have been away from polite Society for far too long, and..." He paused and shook his head, as if he were struggling to come up with the correct words to complete his explanation.

"Away?" Lydia prompted.

The man who had claimed his name was Adonis made eye contact, his brown eyes wide. "Yes," he replied with a slight nod. "On the Continent, in fact," he said in a quiet voice. "I was a... soldier." His gaze dropped to the tulip he held.

Lydia's slight inhalation of breath was barely audible, but she knew he heard it when he lifted his eyes to hers. A warm, rich brown, his eyes still appeared as sad as they had in the dim museum. "So, the scar on your cheek is from a war wound," she guessed in a quiet voice.

Adonis swallowed before allowing a nod. "Indeed. Probably a good thing, though."

Her eyes wide from his odd response, she shook her head. "How can that be? You could have been killed!"

The expression on the knight's face changed in an instant, the sadness gone from his eyes at hearing her words. "Aye," he agreed. *But someone had plans for me.* "My mother wouldn't be too pleased, you see. Always thought I had a perfect face." He sobered. "Can't have her making that claim about me now, which is just as well."

Lydia angled her head to one side. "I've never been a mother, but I rather think she prefers a son with a scar than have you dead from a war wound," she countered.

Adonis allowed a nod, his brows furrowing. "Truth be told, I have no idea of her preferences. She died whilst I was in—"

The two were interrupted when a footman approached with a tray of champagne. Adonis—it was hard for Lydia to think of him as 'Sir Donald'—took two flutes from the tray and handed one to Lydia, not even asking if she wanted one. She thanked him with a nod.

"To new friends?" he offered as he lifted his glass in her direction.

Lydia paused a moment before touching the rim of her glass to his. "New friends," she murmured before taking a sip.

"I'm of a mind to kiss you."

Lydia blinked. And blinked again at the man's bold comment. "Here?" she managed to get out when she found her voice. "Now?" *Faith!* They had just a moment ago been formally introduced, and now he wanted to kiss her! "We've only just…"

Adonis shook his head. "I apologize. I didn't mean it," he claimed suddenly. "I mean, I did mean it, of course. I just didn't intend to say it out loud like that," he added. He took a deep breath and allowed a long sigh. "Now I suppose you'll not accept an invitation to ride with me in the park for fear I'll…" He allowed the invitation to trail off, his eyes downcast.

Having no idea how to respond—everything about the knight seemed odd—Lydia merely allowed a shrug. "Mayhap when the weather improves," she finally replied, managing to make her reply sound encouraging.

The sadness returned to his mournful eyes, his disappointment apparent. "Of course. It is a bit chilly these days." His eyes widened and he held out his champagne glass. "Hold this, please."

Startled, Lydia took the glass and watched in wonder as the knight quickly doffed his topcoat and settled it over her shoulders. The scent of sandalwood and spice cologne wafted past her nostrils, and his blessed warmth, trapped in the superfine of his coat, seeped into her shoulders. "That's very kind of you," she said. "I wore a pelisse, of course, but I left it in the vestibule with the butler. It didn't seem proper to wear it during a garden party," she explained, wondering if she sounded like a ninny. "Seeing as how it's supposed to be springtime and all. I feel rather bad for Lady Morganfield. I know how important this party is to her favorite charity."

Adonis reclaimed his glass from her hand. "Your beautiful gown would have been hidden from view had you worn it," he countered. "On your second day of not having to wear widow's weeds, why, it would have been a shame to leave it covered."

Lydia had to suppress the urge to blink again. How did Adonis know her mourning was over? Before she could wonder too much, she realized Adele had probably said something to the man when he requested the introduction. "Thank you for saying so," she replied before taking a sip of champagne, closing her eyes as the bubbles burst on her tongue and the liquid dribbled down her throat.

There was something positively decadent about drinking champagne in the light of day, out in the open, where anyone could see. A slight buzz seemed to settle in her knees even before she felt it in her head. She wondered how she must look, standing in a secluded part of the garden with a glass of champagne in one hand and a strange man's topcoat draped over her shoulders.

A half-second later, she was wondering far more, for Adonis suddenly leaned forward and kissed her on the corner of her mouth.

Her gaze immediately went to his, her brows furrowing.

There were at least two of three things she probably should have done just then. Admonish the man for having taken advantage—they were out in the open, for goodness sake!—for anyone could have seen him kiss her.

Slap the man across the face—except that to do so might leave another mark on an otherwise almost perfect face.

Or simply take her leave of him and return to the cluster of other matrons who still chatted around a metal lattice table. She would have to give up his topcoat, of course, which may have been part of the reason for her reaction, for Lydia did none of these.

She simply stared at Adonis for a moment, holding her breath when she realized she wanted the sadness gone from his eyes. Another moment passed before she stepped forward and returned the kiss. She didn't place it on the corner of his mouth, though, but directly on his lips. Quickly—just a peck—but a kiss nonetheless.

As she expected, the sadness in his eyes changed to something else. A light seemed to bloom in his irises. Was that hope she saw? Or simply a randy man's realization that he could get what he wanted?

She rather hoped it was the former, for if it were the latter, she would be slapping the man across his almost-perfect face. With any luck, the sapphire on her wedding ring would scrape his left cheek and leave a scar matching the one on his right cheek.

"You honor me, my lady," he murmured, lifting her free hand to his lips.

Lydia was left with the impression that if he hadn't been holding a champagne flute, he might have used the fingers of both his hands to peel the silk glove from hers and have his way with her fingers. Her knuckles nearly jerked at the thought of his lips touching them directly, of what it would feel like to have the firm pillows of his lips make contact for longer than a brief brush-of-a-kiss.

Embarrassed by her actions, Lydia dipped her head. "I am no longer fresh from the schoolroom, but even so, I should not have done that," she whispered.

Adonis allowed a crooked shrug. "Possibly not," he murmured, although Lydia was relieved when the sadness didn't return to his eyes.

Another thought had hers opening wider, though. "Do I have the pleasure of knowing your *wife?*" she asked, sounding prickly again. Part of her hoped he would deny having married while another hoped he had a wife. Then she could admonish him...

Faith! What is wrong with me?

At his violent reaction—the man took nearly an entire step backwards and had to recapture and use his cane to keep from stumbling—Lydia had her answer before he could say, "I don't see how that is possible given there is no Mrs. Truscott," he replied.

Truscott. The name was familiar, but she couldn't place just why at the moment. Rather surprised at the sense of relief she felt, though, Lydia worked hard to keep her expression impassive. "Are you new to London?" she asked, realizing just then that he might have arrived during her mourning period. She certainly hadn't seen him at any *ton* events prior to Jasper's death. Perhaps he had been attending the *ton* events for the past year whilst she had stayed home, minding the dictates that Society placed on widows.

A cloud seemed to pass over Adonis at that moment, his face losing its pleasing expression, his eyes no longer regarding her with the same unwavering interest.

He seemed positively lost in thought.

Lydia glanced around, pretending she didn't notice how he stared into space. She dared a glance to her left, hoping to find Adele hovering somewhere nearby. But the cluster of older matrons no longer circled the ornate table, and the others that had been mingling on the lawn had all disappeared. The impending rain, which had merely threatened in the form of deep gray clouds on the horizon, was about to shower down onto them. Indeed, sprinkles were already leaving water droplets on the brim of Adonis' top hat. A chilly breeze had her shivering despite the topcoat covering her shoulders and back.

Lydia quickly raised her parasol and stepped forward in an effort to provide cover for the both of them. "We need to get inside," she said with some urgency.

Adonis continued to stare at something in his mind's eye, her words having no effect on the man. Threading her free arm around his, she repeated her plea as she gave his arm a tug. His eyes didn't clear, but his legs seemed to finally move, although they did so as if they were made of wood.

"You're scaring me, Sir Donald," she said, wondering what she needed to do to bring him out of his reverie.

What had she said to send him into the trance?

Are you new to London?

That couldn't be what had the man nearly comatose. *Could it?* When he didn't pick up the pace, she moved her hand from his elbow down to his hand. She gripped it, giving it a shake. "Adonis!" she shouted over the sound of the increasing wind and blowing leaves in the nearby shrubs.

Adonis was staring at her, glancing down at how she held his hand, his eyes finally turning up to find her parasol hovering over him, his head angling about as if he were trying to determine where he was.

When he finally returned his attention to her, he lowered his head and closed his eyes. "You should have left me, my lady. You should be inside where it's warm and dry," he murmured, an expression of pain crossing his face.

"I would do no such thing," Lydia argued in a shout. She tugged on his hand again and they hurried to the French doors, Adonis' limp apparent in his broken stride.

Alfred held one of the doors open, an umbrella dangling from one hand as if he had intended to come out to look for them. By the time the two stepped through the doors and into the ballroom, the knight's shirtsleeves were nearly soaked through. The bottom of Lydia's gown was damp, although Adonis' superfine topcoat had kept her shoulders dry.

"Oh, faith, I didn't realize you two were still out there!" Adeline Carlington said as she hurried into the ballroom. "Everyone else has moved to the parlor for the refreshments and music."

Lydia didn't miss the implication of their hostess' words. She had been in the company of Sir Donald—without benefit of a chaperone—for a long time. They had no doubt been missed when the weather turned.

Lydia quickly doffed the topcoat and wrapped it around the knight's shoulders, managing to say, "You'll catch your death," just as the butler removed the man's top hat and offered the two of them bath linens. She turned her attention back to Adeline. "We were having the most pleasant conversation about tulips and didn't even realize it was about to rain."

Adeline glanced at Adonis before stepping up to whisper in Lydia's direction. "Is he well?"

Lydia blinked but managed a slight shrug. "Just a bit soaked from the rain is all," she replied *sotto voce*. She didn't believe her own words though. Something had captured

Adonis' attention, something in his mind's eye. Something so arresting, it had the man's complete and utter attention.

What had Adonis behaving so? Whatever it was, she wasn't about to ask him. He still seemed a bit discombobulated and ever so embarrassed over the matter. In fact, he suddenly pulled a cheque from a pocket inside his damp topcoat and handed it to a rather startled Adeline. "Thank you for the invitation. I really must be going," he said before giving them both a deep bow. Retrieving his top hat from the butler, he quickly took his leave of them.

Alfred, caught unawares, had to hurry to give the man his cane, the accessory pulled from his hand when the butler helped him into his topcoat.

Lydia curtsied and frowned as she watched the knight limp from the ballroom, his boots making uneven tapping sounds on the polished wood and then on the marble tiled floor of the hallway, all the way to the vestibule.

When Lydia was sure he had taken his leave of Carlington House, she turned to her hostess. "I'm not quite sure what just happened, but I couldn't just leave him out there."

"I know, darling. I'm sure no one noticed but you," Adeline said with a wave of her hand. The marchioness took a look at the cheque Adonis had given her and raised an eyebrow. "I will have to be sure Sir Donald is invited to all my charity soirées, though," she said in a hoarse whisper.

"Oh?" Lydia replied, wondering at the comment. When Adeline held out the cheque so Lydia could see the amount written in a bold, even script, Lydia's eyes widened. "Oh, my," she whispered.

Five-hundred pounds!

How could Adonis Truscott afford such a sum? The title of 'sir' implied the man had been knighted for service to Crown and country. He probably wouldn't have earned such a sum from his...

She furrowed her brows. *Soldier.*

Had he been in the army? Or the navy?

The wound on his cheek had been caused by a bayonet, which suggested he could have been in either. Perhaps the man had been an officer. Or perhaps he was the younger son of an aristocrat. How else could he afford such a large contribution to Lady E's 'Finding Work for the Wounded'? Why, five-hundred pounds was enough to cover Lydia's living expenses for nearly two years and pay for an entirely new wardrobe!

"Rather generous of the man," Lydia finally replied with a wan smile. She couldn't help but remember the way his eyes stared into space, though. How blank they had been.

Unseeing.

The marchioness hooked an arm into Lydia's and led her out of the ballroom. When they reached the parlor doors, Adeline made a motion indicating Lydia should precede her into the parlor. "I'm just going to check on the tea and take this to the study," she said as she indicated the cheque.

Lydia acknowledged her comment with a nod and paused before stepping completely into the parlor. Disheartened to see so few women—and even fewer gentlemen—still in attendance, she pasted on a smile and breezed into the room as if she'd merely been detained by their hostess. Hurrying to where Adele sat at the piano-forté—the countess was playing a minuet as the others in the room chatted quietly—Lydia moved to turn the pages of the music.

"Did he leave already?" Adele asked, never taking her eyes from the sheets of music as her long fingers danced over the ivory and black keys.

Lydia nodded. "Quite suddenly, in fact," she replied, not bothering to hide the concern in her voice. She dared a glance at the others in the room, relieved to discover no one seemed to be paying her much attention. Perhaps her delay in making her way into the parlor had gone unnoticed by the other guests.

"I do hope you didn't mind the introduction. I almost didn't grant the man his request, seeing as how I barely know him myself." Adele seemed to concentrate on the sheet of music before adding, "If you'd like, I can ask Grandby what he knows of Sir Donald."

The younger woman arched an eyebrow at this bit of news. She had hoped the knight was an acquaintance of Adele's husband and Lydia's cousin, the Earl of Torrington. She sighed. "I didn't mind, of course, but he is a bit of a chap."

Adele finished the musical selection, and Lydia moved another sheet of music into place. "Well, he is an old fogey," the countess replied, giving Lydia a quick glance before she started to play again.

An old fogey? Well, Adonis was certainly a wounded soldier, Lydia realized, thinking of the scar on his cheek and remembering his noticeable limp.

"According to his sister, he hasn't been the same as before he left for the Continent. That was well over a year ago."

Lydia nearly missed the cue to change the page of the music. "Sister?" she prompted as she quickly turned the page. She wondered if she knew the woman.

"Lady Craven," Adele said with an arched eyebrow.

Her eyes widening in surprise, Lydia had to suppress the gasp she would have allowed had the two of them been alone in the parlor. "He doesn't seem old enough to be her *brother*," she countered in a whisper. Indeed, Persephone Truscott Craven, Viscountess Craven, had to be at least twenty years older than Adonis. Her daughter had married years ago and had three children before illness took her. The oldest son was already at university! Adele's comment suggested she had spoken with Lady Craven recently, but given Viscount Craven's reputation—he was reported to be a gambler of the worst sort—his independent wife took her leave of London on a regular basis and spent most of her time at their country estate in Herefordshire.

"Is she in town now?" Lydia asked in a whisper, leaning down so she could turn the page and be heard over the music put out by the piano-forté.

Adele nodded. "Just a month or so, I believe," she

murmured. "She wanted to attend Huntington's ball and check on Sir Donald. Seems his valet sent word when he became... concerned."

The younger widow wondered if Sir Donald's arrival in London coincided with his sister's, but realized to put voice to another query involving the knight would only lead Adele to believe she had an interest in the man.

Of course, she had no interest in the man.

She had, however, changed her poor opinion of him. Seeing his vacant eyes and then the sudden change in him when he was brought back to the here and now was astonishing. Although it didn't explain his behavior in the museum, something had apparently happened whilst he was away.

Is he staying with his sister in London? Perhaps they had both been at the country estate since Adonis' return from the Continent.

Lydia shook her head as if to clear it. *What does it matter? I am not the least bit interested in Adonis*, she reminded herself.

Adonis.

Sir Donald.

Sighing, Lydia remembered how he looked as they conversed in the garden.

He is a beautiful man, she thought with a sigh. *A beautiful, broken man.*

CHAPTER 8

A BROTHER REPORTS FOR
DINNER WITH A SISTER

*L*ater *that evening*
"You're soaking wet!" Persephone Craven, Viscountess Craven, complained when her brother appeared in the vestibule of her townhouse in Curzon Street.

"Just a bit damp is all," Adonis replied. Rain showered from his hair, dripping down his face and from the shoulders of his topcoat. When a maid appeared with a stack of bath linens, he gave her a nod and helped himself to one. "*Merci*," he whispered, knowing Persephone would scold him for thanking a servant if she overheard the word. The maid gave a surreptitious nod before disappearing.

"Where have you been?" the viscountess asked as she took the linen from his hands and began brushing the water droplets from his topcoat in less than gentle swipes. "I do expect you'll be spending the night here. The weather is a fright. The guest bedchamber is made up and all ready for you."

Once his topcoat was clear of water droplets, Adonis shrugged out of it and allowed his sister to do the same to his waistcoat. He kept hold of his topcoat despite the butler's attempt to take it from him. "I was riding out at the Serpentine," he finally replied, not bothering to add that he had stopped at Carlington House for the garden party on his way home. "Although I appreciate the offer of your hospitality, I do have my own rooms in Green Street. I shan't be spending the night here," he stated, hiding his annoyance at her insistence he take the guest room for the night.

The comment had his sister frowning. "Because you'll be spending the night at Mrs. Gibbons' brothel, no doubt."

Adonis winced, wondering why she would think such a thing. But then he wondered if maybe he had at one time patronized the place and simply didn't remember doing so.

His head was such a muddle these days.

Had he paid a visit to the notorious brothel since his return to London? He was quite sure he hadn't. Why, it had never been his habit to gamble or spend a night with a prostitute before he left for the Continent. Indeed, anything his brother-in-law did had him pursuing the opposite when it came to nighttime activities.

"Never," he finally replied with a shake of his head, rather shocked when he realized his sister mentioned a brothel out loud. And even more shocked that she would accuse him of patronizing one. "I have no desire to go to a brothel or even a gaming hell," he whispered, hoping a servant hadn't overheard Persephone's accusation. "Not all of us are like your husband, after all."

He immediately regretted the comment. Where had it even come from? It was as if he didn't have control of what he said these days, as if he could only speak the truth when he spoke at all. "I apologize. I... I didn't mean that, sister."

Although Persephone should have reacted in horror at his original comment, she merely frowned and rolled her eyes. Everyone in the *ton* knew her husband was a gambler, but that didn't necessarily mean he frequented houses of ill repute. She had long ago ceased to be embarrassed by his actions, though. He had just the year before finished paying off a debt that threatened to send him to prison. "Dinner will be served in a half-hour," she finally said with a sigh, apparently ignoring his comment. "I still need to change. Use the guest chamber at the top of the stairs, and do try to dry off, won't you?"

Adonis nodded, realizing his sister was no longer capable of feeling embarrassment due to her husband's actions. He gave a slight bow and made his way up the stairs to the bedchamber she suggested, glad to find a fire already lit and the room warm.

The guest bedchamber had at one time belonged to his late niece. Given their ages, she had been more like an older sister to him. The thought had him blinking back the sudden image of Elizabeth at her come-out. Resplendent in a white satin gown featuring a sarcenet overskirt in silver, she appeared confident and quite ready to insert herself into the *ton*. Although she hadn't secured an offer of marriage that night, nor any offers the rest of that Season in 1797, Elizabeth had married a banker who was the third son of a duke. She gave birth to three children before pneumonia took her life in 1808. The oldest, a son, was already at university.

Although Adonis had been too young to attend the ball, he had spent the night hiding behind drapes in the grand hall, spying on the array of glittering ladies and their elegantly garbed escorts as they lined up to be announced.

If only he hadn't been discovered by the butler! Off to bed he went, wondering when he would graduate from trousers to the satin breeches so many of the men sported that night. And where was his nephew-in-law now? Somewhere on the Continent with his great nephew and a great niece who was said to be the spitting image of her mother.

Emelia, he remembered, although he had never actually met the young lady.

Adonis shook himself from his reverie, determined to stay in the here-and-now. "Study the room," he said to himself in a whisper.

Decorated with Louis XIV furniture and a plethora of gold velvets and brocades perfectly positioned on a rich Turkish carpet, Elizabeth's bedchamber suggested a level of decadence that couldn't be found anywhere else in the town-house. Although it was easy to imagine spending the night in such fine surroundings, there was another bedchamber in which he would rather spend the night.

That of Lydia Barrymore.

The image of her alone in a bed had his cock coming to life. *At least something of me wasn't damaged on the battlefield,* he thought as he moved to stand before the fireplace.

Mesmerized by the flames, Adonis continued absently drying off his face and clothes with the bath linen. Staring at the flickering fire, it was easy to simply allow his thoughts to drift off, to take him to another place, another time...

He jerked himself out of the beginning of the reverie. That other place wasn't a pleasant place to be, he reminded himself. Indeed, every time he was there, his leg gave him excruciating pain. Every time he was there, someone other than Lydia was there with him.

Allowing himself a moment to remember how she had kissed him, Adonis closed his eyes and allowed the barest hint of a smile to form.

This is better, he thought with a sigh. *So much better.*

A knock at the door brought him out of a memory of seeing Lydia in her sprigged muslin gown, wearing his topcoat, standing on her tip-toes so she could lean in and kiss him. He lifted his topcoat to his face and inhaled, sure her perfume lingered there. He would have to warn his valet not to brush it just yet. *Orange blossoms,* he thought with another sigh. *Orange blossoms and some kind of...*

Another knock, this one more urgent, jerked him back to awareness.

"Come!" he called out, rather annoyed at the inter-ruption.

The butler appeared around the door's edge, his face tinged with worry. "Dinner is served, Sir Donald."

Adonis blinked, shocked to discover the hands on the mantel clock had reached ten past eight o'clock.

Oh, damn it! Persephone would not be pleased. A half-hour had passed without him even realizing it!

"I'll be right down," he replied with a nod.

Pulling on the nearly dry topcoat, Adonis made his way to join his sister for dinner, rather pleased when a waft of orange blossoms drifted past his nose.

CHAPTER 9
AN AGENT REPORTS
FOR DUTY

*E**arlier that afternoon*
Not easily stunned, Matthew Fitzsimmons realized he had experienced two events in the past day that left him feeling at least a bit surprised. First, the unexpected appearance of his wife in his bedchamber last night had him hoping she would visit him again.

Every night.

Second, the unexpected appearance of Donald Truscott that morning, exactly one year to the day of his near fatal mission. Their discussion had the viscount wondering if perhaps the agent wasn't as addled-brained as the man's sister implied.

The third unexpected appearance occurred at precisely four o'clock in the afternoon that same day—the day of Lady Morganfield's garden party.

He knew there was to be a garden party, for his wife had mentioned it that morning, her infectious enthusiasm for the first outdoor event of the Season bringing an unusual smile to his lips. Actually, the smile might have been due to what her fingers were fondling at the time. Anyway, she told him all about the party to be held at Carlington House before she left his bed.

Before she left and took all the warmth with her.

The memory of her luscious body beneath his had helped to rekindle some of the warmth he'd felt upon falling asleep last night. Even now, a sort of glowing ember seemed to be lodged dead center in his chest.

Either that, or he had a case of heartburn from the lunch of cheese and roast beef his clerk had delivered from the Crown and Anchor.

"How do, Chamberlain."

The feminine voice had Matthew glancing up from a rather dull report—some inept analyst's take on the ongoing search for smugglers who were using the Channel to transport illegal liquor. He was forced to blink a time or two, for the woman who stood in his doorway seemed familiar and yet appeared entirely different from when he had last seen her at the theatre not a month ago, garbed in black and hiding behind the netting that decorated the hat she wore. "Lady Barrymore?" he replied, finally standing up.

Lydia waved him down. "No need to stand on my account, my lord," she said as she moved farther into his office. "I know how your knees give you grief." She wore the same gown and hat she had worn to Lady Morganfield's garden party, and although the bottom of the sprigged muslin was still damp from the earlier rain, it wasn't immediately apparent. Her pelisse, folded so the rain-streaked side was on the inside, hung over one bent arm.

"What have you done to look so different?" the viscount asked as he angled his head.

The widow of the late Commander Jasper Barrymore allowed a shrug. "Oh, really, Chamberlain. It's been a year. I am out of mourning. Out of widow's weeds," she replied as she indicated the bright-colored gown. She finally made her way to the chair across from his desk and settled into it, her reticule landing on her lap while a deep green parasol dangled from one wrist. "I am reporting for duty."

Matthew leaned back in his chair, rather stunned by her words. *Jesus!* Despite his meeting with Adonis Truscott that morning—and the reminder of what had happened a year ago—he was still rather surprised by her words.

Had it truly been a year since Barrymore's death?

The older he got, the faster time seemed to fly.

As for her other comment, he cursed himself for not having given much thought as to what he should have her do next.

Although he had some work for a female agent outside of England, he didn't particularly wish to send Lydia Barrymore to do it. She wasn't a classic beauty, but her aristocratic features were hard to hide. Besides, it didn't seem right sending her off to the Continent to infiltrate an illegal liquor trader's firm, nor dispatch her to the Mediterranean to run with the likes of a pirate's crew. If he offered her to the Home Office, they would probably assign her to play someone's mistress in an attempt to discover the brains behind a smuggling operation.

He had half a mind to pension her out of the Foreign Office, but he hated the idea of losing her and her abilities.

How had Jasper Barrymore known to marry her? Did the viscount know beforehand that she was so perceptive? Observant? That she understood motive and intent? Could memorize lines of a code and recite them later? Solve intricate puzzles quickly?

Or had he married her first and then realized how valuable she could be to King and country?

Lydia Barrymore belonged in London. Needed to stay in London. And he had the perfect assignment for her if only he could get her to agree to befriend a fellow agent.

"Very good," he finally responded to her comment about reporting for duty. "I admit, I'm a bit surprised at your return," he finally stated, leaning forward. "Today of all days."

Lydia frowned. "Why is that? You told me to come back in a year."

Matthew sighed before considering how to respond. "It's just..." He allowed a shrug before he pinned her with a steely gaze. "It would be difficult for you to hide your features should I assign you to a smuggling operation."

Rather disappointed at hearing the possible assignment, Lydia still wondered how she might be of assistance. "Would you at least consider dispatching me to do the footwork instead of going to *The Times* for information?" Lydia pleaded, hoping she didn't sound as desperate as she felt just then. She needed an assignment. A distraction. A reason to get out of her bed in the morning, especially given how damned cold it was.

Lord Chamberlain frowned at her query. "I'll be damned if I go to *The Times* for intelligence," he murmured, the viscount displaying a rather sour expression.

Lydia sat very still, aware her comment had touched a sore spot. It was true the newspaper had more investigators, more reporters on the Continent than England had in the way of intelligence officers. They had a bigger budget for news gathering than the Foreign Office had.

"I rather doubt the Alien Office has anything for me, given the situation with France," Lydia commented with a sigh. "But I figured you might." Peace between England and France meant the Alien Office, charged with seeing to the deportation of any immigrants deemed unsuitable to England, was suddenly not as necessary as when French revolutionaries and refugees were pouring in from across the Channel. Their sole purpose these days was to simply deport those they suspected of treasonous activities. Truth be told, peacetime was no panacea for the two agencies.

When the viscount didn't offer an immediate response, she sighed. "Intelligence was probably far easier before seventeen-eighty-two."

Matthew angled his head, remembering the day the Southern Department of the Secretary of State was informed they would be merging with the Northern Department to form the current Foreign Office. He had been a clerk back then—he hadn't yet inherited the Chamberlain viscountcy—and his father wanted him educated in an alternative manner to serve the Crown. He had stayed on despite the merger and been promoted over the years to his current position. What he knew from his work at the Foreign Office certainly made it easier when it came to vote on topics of importance in Parliament.

"I'm not going to send you to the Continent, and I'm certainly not going to let the Alien Office have you," Matthew stated. "Not when I have a situation right here in London."

Straightening in her chair, Lydia nearly held her breath. "Situation?" she repeated, her intrigue apparent.

"How much did you know about your husband?" he asked. He pulled the drawing Adonis had given him earlier that day from beneath a few papers, realizing he winced as he did so.

Sensing a trap, Lydia forced herself to remain calm and display a dispassionate expression. "All the usual, of course. Parentage, age, height, weight, hair color, eye color..." She paused. "What have you there?"

"His position. Did you know what he did before you married him?" Matthew queried, ignoring her question.

Lydia sighed before she dared a look back at the open door. "Which one, Matthew? His position as an officer over an infantry unit during the war?" she hedged, one eyebrow arching in query. "Or...?"

The viscount straightened in his chair and leaned his elbows on the desk. If he was annoyed by her use of his given name, he didn't show it. "The *or*," he said as he lifted his chin.

Glancing back again at the open door, Lydia gave a 'tsk' before getting up and moving to close it.

"What are you doing?"

Lydia waited for the latch to click into place before she angled her head and answered the viscount's query. "Closing the door, of course. There are two clerks out there I've never seen before, and a caddy from the Home Office who looks as if his eyes are about to pop out of his head."

Matthew straightened in his chair, impressed that her attention to detail was still so sharp. "Both clerks are fully vetted and cleared to hear and read classified reports. As for the caddy..." He sighed and rolled his eyes. "Master John is deaf. He shouldn't be a problem—"

"He can *see*, Matthew," Lydia countered as she returned to her seat. "He can probably read lips, too."

The viscount blinked. Damn it, but the woman was suspicious. "Point taken. Now, tell me what you knew."

The widow took a deep breath and let it out before she said anything. "I knew Jasper was one of Wellington's men, of course," she whispered. "And he worked for you when he wasn't reporting to the War Office." She arched an eyebrow. "Or perhaps he *always* worked for you?" This last was said as more of a question than a guess.

Matthew blinked. "Of course he did," he responded, a hint of disappointment apparent in his voice. He handed the drawing across the desk, holding it until Lydia finally reached for it. He watched as she studied the drawing, her gaze taking in far more than just the brutal scene depicted in the middle. He watched as she struggled to retain her composure. At no point did tears brighten her eyes, though.

"A bayonet, then. That's how he died," was all she said. She handed the drawing back to Chamberlain.

"Aye. He was also shot in the shoulder sometime before that."

Lydia sighed. "I'll let his brother know. That is, if you haven't already informed him."

Chamberlain shook his head. "No need to. I'll see Barrymore when I'm next in Parliament," he said quietly. "I am sorry for your loss. For mine as well. He was a good man. A good operative," he said quietly.

"He recruited me, didn't he? Wasn't that why he was dispatched to find and marry me?" Lydia paused a moment. "Did you give him that order, too?"

The viscount cursed as his hand hit the top of his desk, but Lydia remained rock steady as she regarded him. "Really,

Matthew. The man appeared out of nowhere claiming he wanted to court me. Even my father was suspicious, but he wasn't about to turn down an offer of marriage from a fellow viscount." Her eyes widened. "Jasper *was* a viscount, wasn't he?" She could just imagine an entire aristocratic line created for the sole purpose of hiding a spy. Or a family of them!

Matthew rolled his eyes and nodded. "Of course he was a viscount! He was a Barrymore, through and through," he insisted. He paused a moment, considering her earlier comment. "If he recruited you, as you seem to think, it wasn't because he was *ordered* to do so by anyone in this office. The man had a knack for discovering people with certain talents, though, and he recognized yours the first opportunity he had to dance with you. At least, that's what he claimed when he brought word of you to us." He paused a moment. "He did have to marry, though."

Lydia struggled to keep the surprise she felt from showing. "Oh?" 'Have to marry' implied all sorts of not-so-pleasant situations, not the least of which was the need to sire an heir to carry on the viscountcy, something Jasper had never accomplished.

It wasn't exactly for lack of trying, although the opportunities to do so had been few and far between.

"He was always in the company of men. If he ever availed himself of a lady of the evening, no one paid witness to it, and after a time, rumors started circulating..." Chamberlain wasn't surprised to hear her sudden gasp.

"How ridiculous!" Lydia interrupted with a shake of her head. "Jasper wasn't a homosexual," she whispered hoarsely.

Matthew sighed. "*We* know that, but all it took was some gossip monger to suggest otherwise, and suddenly he was under scrutiny."

Sighing, Lydia settled back into her chair. She had always wondered at Jasper's motivation when it came to courting her. To proposing marriage, especially after such a short courtship. "He was a good man, Matthew. A good viscount, too," she added before she was forced to swallow a sudden sob. At some point, she had fallen in love with her husband. Fallen in love and had visions of becoming a mother, of bearing an heir, and a spare, and a daughter or two.

"And since you didn't bear him an heir, his brother now has that honor."

If Lydia felt a sting of guilt or hurt at the accusation, she hid it well. "Seems I'm in good company, though," she countered with an arched eyebrow, her head angling up in defiance.

The viscount understood her meaning immediately, at once angered and then hurt by her words. "Touché," he replied as the entire frame of his body slumped. Despite all the years he and Caroline Harrington had been married, she had never borne him a child. But then, he hadn't exactly been in her company much in the early years, what with travel for his assignments and late nights in Whitehall. Since she was seeing to raising her niece, Samantha, Caroline didn't seem particularly interested in having a child of her own. Perhaps it was time to bring up the topic. Get home a bit earlier. Drop some hints and hope for an invitation to her bedchamber. Do more of what he had done last night, even though he didn't quite know what it was he had done to garner his wife's attentions. To find himself in the same bed with her. To find her suddenly wanton and willing beneath him.

The memory had his cock hardening and his mind on lustful thoughts of his wife.

Lydia felt a hint of satisfaction at how her words had the viscount ruminating. "Although, if you continue what you were doing last night, I should think you'll get a child on her within the year." The statement, made with just a hint of spite, had Lydia regretting it almost immediately. "Oh, dammit. I apologize. That was uncalled for." *Damnation!* What was it about men and their topics of conversation that had her so defensive these days?

Matthew stared at her for a full ten seconds, a series of

possible reasons Lydia could know such a detail ticking off in his brain. "I cannot believe Caro would speak of our..."

Lydia rolled her eyes. "She didn't say a *word*, Matthew. She didn't need to. I can tell when a woman's been tumbled three ways to Thursday." She paused a moment and sighed, rather glad to see his reaction to her comment. Why, she was sure the man was blushing! The curmudgeon was married to one of the friendliest women in the *ton*, and it was obvious he worshipped her. It was past time the two realized they were well-suited for one another. "She was positively *glowing* this afternoon at the garden party. Looked rather youthful, too. And you look as if you might have youthened five or ten years since I saw you at the theatre last month."

The viscount cleared his throat, stunned by Lydia Barrymore's words. He had never known her to be so direct—she rarely put voice to her observations given she usually had to supply them in written reports.

No wonder Jasper had insisted she would make a good agent. A good operative. A better analyst.

Well, at the moment, he didn't need a spy in the field so much as someone to keep an eye on another spy. Or perhaps... he straightened. "Lady Craven has been rather vocal about her brother's bouts of melancholy since his return from Brussels," Matthew stated. "She claims he stares off into space for hours at a time. Called him a Bedlamite in the company of several aristocrats. The man is due to be knighted in the morning..."

Lydia straightened in her chair, well aware of just whom Lord Chamberlain was describing. "Adonis Truscott?" she interrupted. "Sir Donald?"

Matthew Fitzsimmons settled back again, deciding that although he was surprised she knew of Adonis Truscott and his status of an about-to-be-knight, he was also quite sure he sensed something else by the way she said his name. He was, in fact, quite sure he had touched a sore spot.

Well, this is about to become interesting, he thought.

"Know him, do you?" he countered carefully.

Lydia blinked. "Of him. I've... I saw him. Today. He was at Lady Morganfield's garden party this afternoon. Gave her a rather generous cheque for her daughter's charity, and he wasn't even on the invitation list." Inwardly, she cringed. *Why the hell was Adonis at the garden party in the first place?* He had a cheque already filled out for the charity, though. Perhaps he merely wanted to support Lady E's 'Finding Work for the Wounded' and thought to give his cheque directly to Lady Morganfield.

What other reason could he have to be there?

Matthew angled his head at this bit of information, wondering just how generous Sir Donald had been. He didn't know if Adonis Truscott could afford a generous donation to anyone, which had him wondering whose money was behind the cheque.

"I need you to... to meet him. Befriend him. As a colleague, if it becomes necessary. Ensure he stays sane, and if he is insane, bring him back to sanity. Accompany him to..." He paused a moment. "To the theatre. Rides in the park. Balls. *Soirées*. Marry him, if you have to. The man was a crack agent back in the day, and I should hate to lose his services over something awful that happened on a battlefield in the Republic of The Netherlands a year ago."

Lydia blinked—that's when Matthew knew he had dented her armor—before she gave her head a quick shake. "Adonis Truscott is my... *assignment?*"

Matthew nodded, rather liking how she fought to retain a modicum of dignity just then. "Whatever you need to do to get him back on an even keel, you have my permission," he stated with a nod, rather enjoying just how Lydia managed to keep a calm façade when he knew she was positively stunned by his words.

"I suppose challenging him to a duel in Wimbledon Commons isn't an option," she murmured, her manner most deadpan.

The viscount pretended to mull over the idea, wondering why she would say something so unexpected. "He would probably beat you at swords, but my money would be on you with a pistol," he stated, a distinct lack of humor sounding in his voice. "No, Lydia. I want him alive. I want him right as rain. I want him sane."

Lydia stared at the viscount. "Don't make me do this," she whispered as she shook her head. "Matthew, the man is ins ... "

"Oh, so you have met him?" Chamberlain interrupted, his voice taking on a sugary tone. "Kissed him, perhaps?"

It was Lydia's turn to hide her shock. *How the hell does he know such a thing?* For a moment, she thought perhaps he was merely baiting her. She had come straight to Whitehall from Carlington House. When would there have been time for someone to report Adonis' clandestine peck on the corner of her mouth? Or hers on his?

There hadn't been, which meant he was teasing.

Feeling ever so spiteful, Lydia cleared her throat. "He initiated it. I merely..." She sighed and rolled her eyes. So much for hiding her tells. "I admit, I felt a bit sorry for the old fogey. At the time. Now, I don't."

Matthew winced before he shook his head from side to side. *Jesus, but the woman could be an enigma!* And cheeky. *Old fogey?* Well, he had noticed the man's pronounced limp and his need to use a cane when the man had been in the office the day before. *Broken leg*, he remembered from the medical report. Compound fracture. Nearly lost the leg, but some young doctor in Brussels insisted he could save it, and then there was a round of surgeries to ensure Sir Donald could walk again.

Matthew also realized he shouldn't have felt the thrill of victory quite as much as he did just then. But he couldn't help himself. "Lydia, he's an important asset. I want him back, and I want him well. Figure out what's got him stuck in the past and... fix him, won't you?"

The last two words gave her an out, but at that point, Lydia decided to accept the challenge. How hard could it be? A bit of feminine attention. A tumble or two. A serious discussion about service to King and country. A punch to the jaw, and the man would be right as rain.

Well, maybe she wouldn't have to punch the man. Unless he went off into one of his extended visits to the inside of his head. Then she might have to punch him.

Or kiss him, perhaps. Her hand was already thanking her lips for an alternative solution.

She wasn't so sure what her lips thought just yet.

At least she had already spent some time in the man's company. He wasn't a complete unknown. He wasn't a bad sort, either. Wasn't particularly proud. Wasn't particularly meek, either. He was merely... annoying.

At least he was beautiful.

With any luck, she could find out what had him spending hours staring into space. Perhaps make him sane before he drove her insane.

"Just promise me you won't admit *me* to Bedlam when this is over," she murmured before rising.

The viscount allowed a shrug. *Should I?* he nearly murmured, a hint of a grin appearing at the corners of his lips.

Sighing—Lydia was sure he wouldn't answer—she was about to take her leave of Lord Chamberlain's office when he stopped her with the words, "Just one more thing."

She glanced over her shoulder before turning to face him. "Just one?" she repeated, sounding almost surprised.

Matthew ignored the spiteful tone. "Jasper's ring. He wasn't wearing it when he died," he said in a quiet voice as he indicated the drawing on his desk.

Frowning, Lydia merely shook her head. "Ring?" she repeated. Jasper had at least a half a dozen rings... "Oh," she replied, dipping her head. "It's true. He left it behind..." She stopped, her frown deepening. *Jasper must have known he wasn't coming back to British shores. Must have known he wouldn't survive. Damn him.* "It's safe," she said with a shrug.

The viscount stared at her for a moment, as if he were

trying to decide if he should say anything more. "See that it stays that way. Do you... know what he kept inside it?"

Lydia gave a shrug. "Currency. Runes. Rolled up bits of paper. It depended on the assignment, I suppose," she hedged.

"Currency?" Matthew repeated, wondering how Jasper Barrymore might have hidden money in such a tiny compartment beneath a fake diamond mounted on a thick gold band.

"Sapphires," Lydia stated as she opened the door. "Universal currency, wouldn't you agree? Now, are you going to promise me you won't admit me to Bedlam when this is all over?"

Matthew finally allowed a grin and was pretending to mull over her request when an ink pen sailed past within an inch of his ear. Had she wanted it to, it would have impaled his eye. "I promise!" he called out as he heard her leave the outer office.

His grin widened to the point where he no longer had the desire to continue working just then. Not when the memory of his wife's soft body beneath him had him imagining how they might warm up the bed on this night.

Helping himself to his greatcoat, he took his leave of Whitehall and hurried home to Fitzsimmons House.

CHAPTER 10

AN INTRUDER IS DISCOVERED

n the middle of the night
The sound of soft snoring brought Lydia out of a fitful sleep. She blinked awake and stared at the canopy above her, barely making out the gathered folds that splayed out from where brocade fabric met at the apex. The canopy curtains draped down to hide the end of the bed as well as the side facing the door to her bedchamber. The side facing her dressing table, the fireplace, and the single window remained open, though, presumably to allow the heat from the fireplace to warm the bed. Only a few embers of coal remained lit, though, and the chilly air had her shivering.

Holding her breath and lying as still as possible, she listened intently.

Her attention went to the window when the soft snore sounded again. Silhouetted against the bit of light that made its way through the window was the shape of a man seated in the room's Greek lounging chair. He was obviously asleep, but the realization did little to slow the pulse she felt pounding in her ears nor prevent the sudden alarm she felt.

How the hell did I sleep through the sound of someone making their way into my bedchamber?

Sliding her hand beneath the pillow next to the one on

which her head rested, she felt for the cold metal of the muff flintlock pistol she kept there. She pulled it out at the same time as she sat up, attempting to straighten her nightrail. The lawn had become twisted around her legs whilst she slept. She moved to get out of the bed, hoping she could do so without making a sound. The ropes beneath the mattress protested the strain, though, and the man's snoring suddenly ceased.

Knowing she would have the upper hand if she could prevent the intruder from standing up, she rushed to stand before him, her nightrail-clad body slightly angled in the event he made to launch himself from the lounging chair. She drew back the hammer on the top of the mock ivory and gold-toned pistol, her thumb steady as she did so, and aimed it at his forehead. She was careful to remain out of his reach, just in case he leaned forward with the intent of launching himself out of the lounging chair to tackle her. "Do not move, or you shall have a hole in your head," she warned in a hoarse whisper.

"I mean you no harm." The simple words were said as his hands slowly came up, their palms facing Lydia. "Quite the opposite, in fact," he murmured.

Maintaining her stance and the aim of the gun, she took a breath. The scent of the man's cologne was barely there, somewhat familiar but not enough to have her guessing whom he might be. "Then why are you here?"

"I am... keeping a promise, my lady," he murmured. "Although, it's become quite evident you can see to your own protection, I suppose."

Lydia frowned, rather surprised by his words and the sound of disappointment she heard in them. "To whom did you make the promise?"

Even before the words were out of her mouth, she realized Jasper had to have been the one to extract such a promise from someone. A fellow officer, no doubt. An officer or a colleague.

An agent.

Slowly lowering the pistol, Lydia stared at the intruder. "When?" she whispered. *Jasper's been dead a year now, but who else could he mean?*

"A year ago. I apologize for the delay. I have not been in London long, and it took some doing to find you…"

Lydia inhaled sharply as she finally recognized the man's voice. "Sir Donald?"

"Well, not yet, but I am at your service, my lady."

A dozen thoughts vied for attention just then—but outrage won out over all the rational reasons. "How *dare* you come into my house? To my bedchamber?" she whispered hoarsely. "Are you *insane?*" The word was out of her mouth before she could censor it, before she realized just how fitting it was to describe Adonis Truscott at that moment. She had been warned, though. Lord Chamberlain had implied the man wasn't in his right mind when she met with him.

"I have been told I am," Adonis acknowledged with a nod, his admission sounding ever so reasonable. "But I dared only because it was a requirement to accomplish what I promised to do." He paused a moment, his head dipping. "As for my presence in your bedchamber… I am not sure where else I could be. I can assure you I was not seen when I came into the house, though."

Lydia blinked, her shoulders slumping as she considered his explanation. He sounded sane. He sounded perfectly reasonable, in fact, even if his actions were the very height of impropriety.

Before she could form a suitable response, she realized her bare feet were freezing despite the rich carpet beneath them. Once that thought had registered, she was aware of how her nipples had puckered into hard buds behind her nightrail, of how her fingers felt chilled. Her attention still on her intruder, she realized he had to be cold, too. He wasn't wearing a greatcoat over his… she wasn't even sure what he was wearing, its dark fabric blending into the chair's uphol-stery in the dim light. "How did you get here?"

It was Sir Donald's turn to blink. "I walked."

Well, at least there isn't a horse parked outside the townhouse, she thought with a bit of relief.

"Got in through the back door, no doubt," Lydia murmured, remembering how the lock was broken.

"Yes, my lady. You really should see to its repair."

Lydia frowned at the familiar annoyance she felt toward the man just then. Could he be any more annoying? "No doubt," she finally responded with a roll of her eyes, not bothering to add that one was scheduled to see to the problem later that day. She crossed her arms in front of her chest, making sure the pistol was uncocked as she did so. The movement had her nipples pressing into the fine lawn of her nightrail, their silhouettes evident despite the dim light from the window. "Can you leave now, please? As you can see, there's really no need for your presence here. I am freezing, and I'd really like to get back to my warm bed."

The gun no longer a threat, Adonis stood up from the Greek lounging chair. "I cannot, my lady," he whispered, shaking his head. "Please, don't make me." He moved to stand directly in front of her, so close, the scent of his cologne was readily apparent.

Stunned by his words, Lydia stared up at him. "You cannot stay here. The gossip—"

"No one will know I am here. I promise," he interrupted, his gaze dropping from her eyes to where her breasts were made evident by her crossed arms.

"*I* will," she countered indignantly.

He reached out, the back of one of his fingers brushing the side of one fabric-covered breast. Lydia jerked at the sensation, both because his finger was cold and because the caress set off a rather pleasant sensation just beneath her skin. "How dare you?" she whispered.

Adonis didn't seem to hear her, for his gaze was entirely on the spot where his finger had touched. Glancing down to see what had his attention, Lydia let out a gasp and changed the angle of her arms to cover the evidence of her chilled nipples. When Adonis didn't seem to notice—indeed, he still stared at exactly the same spot—Lydia sighed. "You're doing it again," she accused. "Staring at nothing..." She allowed her words to trail off when she realized he was somewhere—or some *when*—else, and probably couldn't hear a word she said. She had half a mind to shove him just to discover if he would topple over or awaken with a start and catch himself. Then she remembered he walked with a limp and decided he would probably topple over either way.

I'm not that cruel.

Weary and cold, she made her way to the bed and slowly settled into it, covering herself against the chill in the room as she continued to keep her gaze on the strange man. Despite her attempt to keep her eyes open, though, she soon drifted off to sleep.

A sob had Adonis straightening, his attempt to breathe interrupted by something apparently lodged in his throat. Aware his cheek was wet, he moved a hand up to determine the source of the moisture, his gaze turning up as if he thought it was rain before his mind finally registered that he wasn't outside. He swallowed the lump in his throat as he realized the cause—tears fell from his eyes.

Poor Johanna!

The unfamiliar surroundings had him glancing about, his gaze finally resting on the counterpane-covered mound on the bed.

Lydia, he thought then with a great deal of relief. Unlike Johanna, she was alive. She was well.

She was angry with him, too, but it couldn't be helped. He had a promise to keep. A duty to perform.

A shiver reminded him it was cold in the room. Moving to the fireplace, he found the tongs the maid used to load coal into the box. Adding the three lumps that had been left on the hearth, he felt a good deal of satisfaction when a flame finally erupted and warmth seemed to penetrate the chill. He dared a glance back at the bed, relieved to see that Lydia still slept. When his shivering ceased, he returned to the uphol-stered Greek lounging chair and settled himself for the rest of the night.

CHAPTER 11
PONDERING AN ENIGMA

The following morning, June 19, 1816

Lydia awoke with a start, sure she felt movement in her bedchamber.

"Morning, milady," Rachel called out from where she was opening the drapes.

Glancing about the part of the room she could see from the open side of the bed, and the amount of light that filtered through the Austrian sheers that still covered the window, Lydia realized it was later than usual. "What time is it?" she asked as she sat up in bed, one hand moving to push the errant locks of hair from her face.

"Nearly nine o'clock, milady."

Nine? A vague memory niggled at the edges of her consciousness. Moving her hand beneath one of the pillows, she felt the cold metal of her gun and relaxed. A quick glance at the Greek lounging chair near the window assured her no one had been sitting in it recently—the seat cushion was smooth.

"Musta been a vera cold night, seein' as how the coal I left on the hearth has been used. Hope it wasn't too much of an inconvenience for you to have to do that yourself," she added with a worried look.

Lydia blinked as she gazed at the palm of her right hand.

There was no evidence of coal dust on her fingers. "Not at all," she murmured, quite sure she hadn't been the one to feed the dying fire.

The memory of Adonis Truscott sitting on the Greek chair beneath the window came flooding back. The memory of her aiming her muff pistol at him. Her threats. His replies.

His lack of reply.

His assurance he wouldn't be discovered.

Well, it was quite evident he hadn't left any evidence of his presence behind, at least in this room, Lydia realized, her quick assessment assuring her that even his boot prints couldn't be found in the Aubusson carpet.

Damn, but the man was an enigma. He hadn't answered the most important question she had asked last night, and yet she had been too tired and too angry to force the answer out of him. She had a gun to his head, for God's sake!

To whom had be promised to provide her protection?

Jasper came to mind, of course. But how? And when?

She was about to spend some time puzzling it out when she realized Rachel was giving her an expectant look. "Just a round gown for the morning. I'll be paying calls this afternoon, though," she murmured. "I'll need the town coach and a driver." A thought to visit the Foreign Office in Whitehall crossed her mind—she had a mind to apprise Lord Chamberlain as to what had happened the night before —but to do so meant she might have to ride in a hackney to get there. No one in her household knew of her prior work for Chamberlain. Even if most of her duties involved reading reports and news sheets or decoding messages from operatives, she preferred her work be kept as secret as possible.

Perhaps she *could* have her driver take her in the town coach when next she paid a visit on Lord Chamberlain, though. There were other buildings in Whitehall she could claim were her destination.

"I'll get some more coal right quick and be back up to help you dress," the maid stated as she headed for the door.

Lydia held up a hand. "While you're down there, could you find out if the back door lock has been repaired yet?"

Rachel's eyes widened. "Of course, milady," she said as she bobbed a curtsy and disappeared with the coal can.

Adonis had made his way into the house via the back door. Lydia was sure of it. What if he had been the one to damage its lock in the first place? As the means to ensure he could gain access to the house and use the back stairs to reach her bedchamber?

Damn him! she thought in dismay.

Well, the sooner the lock was repaired, the better. If Adonis Truscott paid her another nocturnal visit, she would know it was because he broke the lock again.

CHAPTER 12
A BROTHER-IN-LAW ISN'T CONVINCED

few hours later

"I think he's worse now than he was when he returned from Europe," Persephone Craven complained in a whisper, arching an elegant eyebrow as she made the comment.

"Now, now, don't exaggerate, m'dear," her husband replied, his attention on that morning's edition of *The Times*. The newly ironed paper had been delivered by the butler only moments before.

Although he hadn't been present in the breakfast parlor that morning, Robert Craven made his way straight to the dining room when he did make an appearance at the Craven townhouse at precisely one o'clock in the afternoon. He immediately took a seat in the large carver at one end of the mahogany table and settled in as if he expected luncheon to be served momentarily.

Persephone struggled to hide her surprise, both because she hadn't expected him and because he didn't smell of having spent the morning in a traveling coach.

Or a gaming hell.

"I assure you, I am not exaggerating," she replied from the other end of the table. The sudden unexpected appearance of her brother, Adonis, had her pasting on a smile. "So glad you could join us, Donald. I wasn't sure you would," she said in an attempt to cover her surprise at having Adonis show up in the dining room only moments after her husband had taken his seat.

Adonis gave Persephone a quelling glance. "I'm quite sure I accepted your invitation for luncheon last evening. Before I took my leave of you," he said before stopping to give his brother-in-law's shoulder a quick shake. "Good afternoon, Craven. Anything interesting in the news today?"

Persephone struggled to keep her mouth closed. She didn't remember asking him to luncheon whilst they shared dinner the night before.

Adonis' manner as well as his query seemed entirely normal to the viscount. "Lord Reading's nag won another race," he replied, finally lifting his attention from the paper to find Adonis taking a seat halfway down the table. A footman was quick to add a place setting and pour wine. "There are reports that red snow is falling in Italy. And it sounds as if the Carlton Group will pursue their project up in Leeds once the canal is complete."

Adonis angled his head. News of red snow falling in the higher elevations of Italy had been reported several times that year. He decided to instead ask about the project in Leeds. "Did you join the investment group?"

Craven shook his head. "The buy-in is entirely too rich for me. If I had that much blunt, why I would use it to play faro at the Jack of Spades. At least then I could be assured of some kind of return on my money," he claimed with a roll of his eyes.

"Faro does favor the player," Adonis commented, his manner not the least bit judgmental. Knowing how poorly his brother-in-law played the card game had him deciding it was a good thing Lord Craven didn't have the money to do so. "But I haven't had the chance to try my luck since I was in Brussels." He frowned before he turned his attention to his sister. "Will you be paying calls this afternoon, my lady?"

Persephone blinked and stared at her brother for a

moment. Perhaps her husband was right. Adonis' behavior seemed entirely... normal. "Given this ghastly weather, I think not," she replied, not meaning her words to sound as prickly as she felt just then. Robert Craven hadn't graced their townhouse with his presence in nearly three days, and then he had simply showed up for luncheon as if he did so every day.

"How was your trip to Sussex?" Adonis asked then, turning his attention back to his brother-in-law.

"Dreary and cold," Craven replied with a frown. "But Cunningham and Waterford know what they're doing. Since Gregory Grandby won't take me on as a client, I figure Cunningham is my next best opportunity to make some blunt this year. Given they have some gypsum mines and how much construction has been going on, I can't help but think there is some money to be made."

"You won't have to pay taxes on your earnings," Adonis said in response.

The viscount lifted his head from the paper and regarded his brother-in-law. "Come again?"

Adonis managed a shrug. "The income tax has been repealed. You won't be taxed for any income you make from a venture with Cunningham and Waterford," he stated.

Craven gave his wife an arched brow before turning his attention back to Adonis. "Good point," he countered. "We had to turn off the spigot, you see, or Prinny would have continued to bleed us dry."

Persephone frowned as she listened to her brother and husband exchange words. She recognized the names he had mentioned. Cunningham was Michael Cunningham, the son of a viscount and an investor with his father-in-law, Harold Waterford, in a variety of business pursuits in the Horsham District of Sussex. The two had investments in ironworks as well as gypsum mines. Given the extreme weather all of England had been experiencing this past winter as well as the wet, cold spring, though, she figured coal mines would be a better investment. At least, as long as people could afford to buy it.

Ever since Sir Humprey Davy had proven his Davy's lamp in the Durham Coalfield earlier that year, coal mines throughout England had begun outfitting their miners with the lamps. She rather imagined Waterford and Cunningham had done the same with the gypsum miners in Sussex. She hoped they hadn't increased the price of their product to compensate for the added expense, though. Most in England could barely afford to buy food let alone mined products.

As for Gregory Grandby, he was a younger cousin of Milton Grandby, Earl of Torrington, and he was a master at investing monies to build wealth for his clients.

"You were in Sussex?" she asked of her husband, not bothering to hide her surprise. Here she had thought he was merely holed up in a gaming hell, gambling away what little was left of the Craven fortune.

Or worse.

Craven gave a shrug in response. "Just returned a few minutes ago," he replied. "I apologize for not sending word of my delay. I truly thought I would be back last night, but the damned roads were so muddy, the coach couldn't get through," he complained. He didn't add that he had spent the night in a coaching inn in Coulsdon.

"I had no idea you had business in Sussex," Persephone countered, wondering why he hadn't let her know of his plans. She had even entertained a thought that he was ensconced in a brothel these past few days.

The viscount frowned. "I left a note for you on your escritoire," he replied, glancing up from the paper to give her a nod. "You were sound asleep when I left, and I didn't have the heart to wake you."

Persephone blinked. And blinked again. Well, she supposed she might have discovered the note if she had bothered to pay a visit to her salon anytime in the last few days. "That was rather considerate of you," she managed in reply, just as the footman delivered a bowl of steaming fish soup in front of her.

Her husband's attention was back on Adonis. "What is it?" he asked, noticing how Adonis seemed deep in thought.

"It makes no sense, of course," Adonis replied with a frown, leaning to one side as his soup was delivered.

"No sense?" Craven repeated.

"The country is eight-hundred and thirty-four million pounds in debt. Why would the income tax be repealed at a time when it is most needed?"

The viscount blinked before finally giving a shrug. "Well, we did have a discussion on the matter in Parliament," he replied, ignoring the bowl of soup that appeared next to his newspaper. "But considering who is saved from having to pay the income tax, it makes perfect sense we would repeal it." The comment came with an arched eyebrow, as if everyone should guess that those in power—those who earned the most money in England—benefited the most from the legislation.

"I take your meaning," Adonis said with a nod, his frown deepening.

"By the way, your sister thinks you're a candidate for Bedlam," Craven stated, his tone most unapologetic. He ignored Persephone's gasp of shock. "What say you?"

Adonis gave the comment some consideration before he allowed a shrug, his brows furrowed so a vertical line appeared between them. "I suppose there are days when it appears as if I probably should be admitted as a patient," he allowed. "But, for the most part, I am sane. Just a bit... *preoccupied* is all," he admitted with a shrug. He didn't add that his most recent thoughts had him imagining Lady Barrymore kissing him again.

In his home.

In his arms.

In his bed.

"What has you *preoccupied?*" Persephone asked from her end of the table.

Her brother allowed a shrug, realizing he couldn't exactly tell her the truth. Well, he could, but then she really would have him admitted to Bedlam. "I discovered only yesterday that I was to be knighted this morning, so there was an investiture ceremony, with all the pomp and..."

Robert Craven dropped his newspaper. "You're a knight now?" he half-questioned, beating Persephone's attempt at stating her disbelief. "Good God, I must not have been in Parliament the day knighthoods were discussed. Either that, or Prinny did it without our approval, which I wouldn't put past him," he added, *sotto voce*. "Well deserved, though, I should think, given your participation in the Battle of Ligny. Congratulations," he added before finally turning to his soup.

"You don't *believe* him, do you?" Persephone countered, her attention on her husband and her pointed statement proving she didn't believe Adonis' comment about his investiture. "I told you he was insane!"

Having reached into a pocket in his topcoat even before Persephone put voice to her protest, Adonis pulled out the badge he had been given during the ceremony. The ribbon on which it was strung trailed behind. "It's rather more heavy than I imagined," he said as he handed the medal to his brother-in-law.

Lord Craven examined the badge and let out a slow whistle. "I suppose now I have to address you as Sir Ad—"

"Donald," Adonis put in abruptly. "But, no, you needn't address me as such." He turned to his sister and was about to say something more when he instead simply sighed and went back to eating his soup.

He was quite sure she was about to faint. If she did, he didn't want to pay witness to her tumble from the table.

"You'll have to forgive your sister, Donald. She's merely concerned since you've seemed a bit... *off* these past two months," Robert said in a soft voice.

"Oh, I have been off," Adonis acknowledged with a nod, not the least bit embarrassed at admitting it.

Off in another place.

Off in another time.

Off-kilter.

Lost.

Robert gave his wife a pointed glance. "Well, as long as you don't go off killing someone, or showing up in some poor woman's bedchamber uninvited, I suppose all is well."

Adonis blinked, wondering why Lord Craven would mention the latter.

Or the former, for that matter.

He had only ever killed four men, all of them French, including the soldier who had used his bayonet in an attempt to kill him first. But how did Craven know he had been spending his nights seeing to Lady Barrymore's protection? "And if I am?" he countered, leaning back as a footman delivered a plate of steaming pork loin swimming in gravy.

Craven regarded his brother-in-law with an arched brow. Then he burst into laughter, the throaty sound eliciting another gasp from his wife. "Carry on, dear brother. Carry on," he replied with a huge grin.

Persephone Craven stared at her plate and allowed a sigh, deciding her husband would never believe her claim.

Perhaps Adonis was more sane than she thought. *Or perhaps it is merely* me *who is losing my grip on reality*, she considered as she stabbed her fork into the pork.

CHAPTER 13
A FORMER LOVER PAYS A
VISIT

An hour later ...

Oliver Preston stepped down from his Irish walker and regarded the townhouse his fellow agent and one-time friend had purchased on the occasion of his marriage to Lydia Grandby. Although its exterior looked like any of the others along Bruton Street—white with Palladian windows, columned porticos over the front doors, and curved wrought iron railings in front of the second- and third-story windows—he thought it much grander on the inside.

Especially one particular bedchamber.

He tossed a coin to a boy who ran up to take the reins of his horse. "Much obliged, guv'nor," the urchin said as he lifted his cap.

Oliver was about to warn the boy he might be awhile, but realized that he was probably already being spied on by at least a few of Lydia's neighbors. If he stayed too long, Lydia would be the subject of rumors and gossip for a fortnight. Better that he state his business and hope she could provide answers quickly. Make it appear as if he were an old family friend merely checking on her well-being.

The visit from Adonis Truscott convinced him he had to finish his business in London and leave—as soon after the wedding as he could manage the arrangements.

The blue painted front door opened before he could use the lion-head knocker. "Mr. Preston for Lady Barrymore," he said as he paused before the threshold. He held out a white pasteboard card, his name engraved in black ink.

Jenkins gave a nod and stepped aside. If he was displeased by the appearance of a man who had paid calls on his master in the past, he didn't show it. "I'll see if Lady Barrymore is in residence," he said before heading down the central hall from the vestibule.

When he had called on the widow in the past, Oliver usually let himself in the back door, crept up the stairs, and went straight to her bedchamber. Lydia was, he had decided, a bit of a prude, insisting she'd rather not have her servants know of her *affaire* with him. *They'll gossip with the neighbor's servants, and should Lady Pettigrew discover I'm...*

A widow having an affaire? he had countered. *You would be gossiped about should you* not *take a lover, dear Liddy.*

Well, today's visit would be brief and to the point. He had to find Jasper's ring.

"Oliver?" The feminine voice held as much surprise as it did welcome.

"In the flesh," he replied as he gave a bow. Rather than kissing the back of her hand, he bussed her on the cheek, making sure the butler noticed. "I thought to check on you whilst I'm still on these shores."

Lydia angled her head and turned to lead him to the parlor. "Can you bring a tea tray, Jenkins?" she said as an aside before turning her attention back to Oliver. "Where will your travels take you this time?"

Her visitor took in a breath and waited as Lydia settled herself into the middle of a dark blue velvet settee. "The Continent is all. The wedding trip," he added a bit sheepishly, thinking she probably didn't want to hear the reason.

"You needn't be apologetic about getting married, Oliver," she scolded gently. "But I must admit, I'm rather surprised it's taken this long for you to find a wife."

He gave a shrug. "One has to *look* for a bride to find

one," he countered, as if his words held some deeper meaning. "I've just never looked before." *Never had to.* He dared a glance toward the door. "Truth be told, I'm getting out of the service completely," he whispered. "I just have this one assignment to complete, and then I'll be wed and off to the Continent."

Lydia didn't have a chance to respond to this news before Jenkins appeared on the threshold with the tea tray. "Do you take milk or sugar?" she asked, giving a nod to Jenkins before he took his leave of the parlor. She knew he preferred the Highland Park scotch Jasper favored and had kept stocked in the study prior to his death, but she wasn't about to offer him a drink in the middle of the day.

"Yes to both," Oliver replied as he leaned forward. Lowering his voice, he said, "I'm afraid my one loose end has a bit to do with Jasper."

Glancing up from the cup she was setting onto a saucer, Lydia regarded her guest with an arched brow. "Oh?"

"I can't give you the details, of course, but I was wondering if I might be allowed to go through his personal effects. The things he had with him whilst he was in that last battle on the Continent."

Handing him the cup of tea, Lydia's expression saddened. "Oh, I'm afraid that's not possible."

Oliver blinked. "Why ever not? I just need to *look*, Liddy," he insisted, his manner hinting at annoyance.

"I haven't yet *received* his personal effects," Lydia remarked, wondering at the sudden sense of unease she felt in the man's presence. He had visited her bed on several occasions. He wasn't the accomplished lover she had hoped for when she accepted his overtures. Although his dark, dangerous looks would have suggested a man who could please a woman between the sheets, he was rather quick with his tumbles, and despite a mouth with lips that promised he would enjoy kissing, he eschewed the practice.

Well, except when it came to her nipples.

Then he seemed to use them liberally. Too bad he hadn't

figured out how to use them to their best advantage. "I have asked at the War Office, of course, but..." She shrugged before seeing to her own cup of tea. "Was there something in particular you were looking for? Perhaps he didn't have it with him over there. Truth be told, I've begun to think he knew he wouldn't be coming back to these shores when he received that last assignment from Wellington."

The dark, handsome man shook his head. "I'm quite sure he would have had to have it with him. A means to pass along... information," he hinted, one of his eyebrows arched up. "Something with a very small compartment. A small pocket watch or... a ring or... a snuff box, perhaps."

Lydia shook her head, careful not to give away the moment she felt alarm at hearing the word 'ring.' She had just discussed the matter with Lord Chamberlain the day before. Caution kept her from offering the details of what she knew about how Jasper hid little bits of information. Tiny folded squares of paper. Gemstones. Thin rolls of papers with a column of numbers penciled onto them. Runes. All of them fit into one particular piece of jewelry he owned. A piece that wasn't particularly well hidden in his master bedchamber. That was the beauty of it, of course. No one thought to look at items that were out in the open or easily discovered in the top tray of a jewelry box.

Lydia shook her head as she pretended to think. "Not a snuff box, certainly. He never used the stuff, and I don't believe he's ever received one as a gift," she remarked before taking a sip of tea. "Perhaps you would have more luck at the War Office than I did," she suggested. "I'm quite sure they only saw me as the grieving widow. Why, I should think they would be more forthcoming should *you* make the request."

Oliver seemed to consider her words before he drained his tea cup. "If you don't mind, I think I will do just that," he replied, moving to stand up.

"Must you go so soon?" Lydia asked, feigning disappointment. "You haven't even eaten a piece of cake."

He seemed to think on the offer before shaking his head.

"Thank you, milady, but no. If I head for the War Office right now, I might make it whilst there's still a clerk or two about," he said as he gave a bow.

Lydia didn't bother getting up, but allowed him to brush his lips over the back of her hand. "Do let me know what you find out, won't you?" she said quietly. "Before you take your leave of these shores?"

Oliver regarded her with a sigh. "I will, Liddy. Do take care of yourself, won't you?"

With that, Oliver Preston gave a leg and took his leave of the townhouse, a plan forming in his mind's eye.

CHAPTER 14
A RIDE IN THE PARK

ater that afternoon

"Would you like to wear your green riding habit? Or the blue one?" Rachel asked as she held up the two choices for her mistress to consider.

Lydia blinked. "Am I going riding?" she countered, her brows furrowing as she dared a glance at the window. Although it wasn't raining at the moment, it was still a rather gray day. She couldn't remember an invitation from anyone to ride during the fashionable hour. Indeed, she had merely come to her bedchamber with the thought of retrieving the book she had started reading the night before.

Anything to get her mind off what she was supposed to be doing.

Befriend him, Lord Chamberlain had said.

Every time she thought of Adonis Truscott, she felt annoyance mixed with pity. How was she to forge a believable friendship from that? And figure out what had the fellow agent prone to extended periods spent in a stupor?

She certainly hoped the viscount had been joking when he mentioned marrying the odd man.

The most surprising aspect of the meeting, though, had been to learn that Adonis Truscott had been serving as an agent under Lord Chamberlain in the first place. Nothing about the man suggested he had skills as a spy...

She suddenly remembered last night. How long had Adonis been in her bedchamber before she realized he was there? He had managed to sneak in and sleep in her bedchamber without anyone in the household knowing!

Lydia stared at her reflection in the looking glass above the dressing table. Could anyone tell *she* was an employee of the Foreign Office just by looking at her?

Of course not.

Rachel's eyes widened at her mistress' query about going on a ride. She dared a glance out the window to her right. "The groom certainly thinks so, my lady. He's just finished saddling your horse and is about to bring it around to the front of the house."

The widow wondered if she had accepted an invitation without remembering having done so. *Not possible,* she thought. More likely that someone had sent one, and she hadn't yet opened it. "The blue one," she announced, deciding that despite the chill in the air and the gray clouds that shrouded the city, she would go riding.

Her mount, a Welsh pony on the taller side, would appreciate the exercise, and frankly, she needed some air. After the incident at Lady Morganfield's garden party and her trip to Whitehall the day before, she hadn't left her townhouse in Bruton Street.

"Would you like me to redo your hair?" Rachel asked when she finished fastening the skirt and doing the buttons up the front of the habit.

Lydia regarded her reflection in the cheval mirror. Although her hair had been done in a simple top-knot, the ringlets Rachel had ironed into it were still coiled at her temples. "No need. The hat will cover most of it." She didn't want the maid's efforts wasted. More rain was expected given the cloud cover, and Lydia rather doubted she would be back at the townhouse before it started to shower.

Rachel was quick to pull a blue velvet and peacock-feather-trimmed hat from the dressing room. Within minutes, she had it pinned securely in place and was admiring Lydia's reflection in the looking glass when there was a knock at the bedchamber door.

Lydia frowned as Rachel hurried to answer the door. The butler, his hands clasped behind his back, stood just beyond the threshold. "What is it, Jenkins?" she asked, leaning over on the dressing table seat so she could see the butler.

Clearing his throat, Jenkins stated, "The escort for your ride has arrived, my lady."

Escort?

Well, if the escort wasn't simply her groom, she would know she had missed an invitation. Lydia added one more pin to her hat and replied, "Then I suppose I am ready as well."

The butler gave a nod before heading back down the stairs. Lydia followed after a moment, rather happy someone had seen to it she had an invitation to ride in the park.

Adele, perhaps?

She rather enjoyed spending time in the company of her newest cousin, the Countess of Torrington. Or mayhap one of the other ladies at the garden party had made the arrangements when she was still in the gardens with Sir Donald. Or perhaps Lord Chamberlain had requested that his wife ride with her.

Lydia was nearly to the bottom of the stairs when she sensed she was being watched. Slowing her descent, she was stunned to discover Sir Donald regarding her from the vestibule, his top hat tucked under one arm whilst he leaned heavily on his cane.

Oh, dear, she thought, realizing almost immediately that she would not be riding in the park with Adele, or Caroline, or with any other of the female acquaintances from the garden party.

Adonis Truscott meant to escort her.

She wondered if Lord Chamberlain had put him up to it.

The cur.

"Why, this is a surprise," she managed, allowing a smile to touch her lips. She hadn't yet decided if it was a good one, but there was no need to give the man the cut direct. They had been properly introduced, after all. She hadn't shot him when she had the chance. And she was supposed to befriend him.

Adonis bowed and reached for her hand even before she had an opportunity to offer it or to even curtsy. Her gloves still clutched in her other hand—she had intended to pull them on in the vestibule—meant Adonis kissed her bare knuckles. Once again, the strange shock waves she felt when he last kissed her hand shot up her arm to nearly her elbow.

"I do hope it's not an unpleasant surprise, my lady," the knight replied, his happy demeanor suddenly darkening. "I was sure I made mention of it..." His voice trailed off, as if he just then realized that he might have imagined making the engagement.

Lydia angled her head, still not sure what she thought of the unexpected arrival of Sir Donald. "Not at all," she managed, wondering if she should be more concerned than she felt just then. "Was there a particular reason you intended to ask me?" she asked as she moved into the vestibule.

Although she didn't know how she would have responded to his invitation during the garden party—especially given how the man's attention seemed lost for so long—she was quite sure she would have shot him last night had he brought up the idea then. Rather than protest, she decided to go along with his plans. With him making the first move, she was saved from having to arrange what might be an even more awkward meeting. Whatever would she use as an excuse to see him?

Adonis seemed to stiffen at the query. "Truth be told, I am not sure, my lady," he stammered. "But I should like you to think me a... a friend, and to do so requires we spend some time in one another's company." He captured his lower lip with a tooth, as if he were trying to recall a missing memory. "If it's an inconvenience, we can certainly do it another day."

Lydia allowed a sigh, rather surprised at his words. *I should like to think me a friend.* If that were truly the case, then perhaps her orders from Lord Chamberlain wouldn't be so impossible. Besides, something about him had her... curious.

Yes, that's what it was.

Curiosity.

Perhaps an hour or two in his company would allow the man to clear up some of the misgivings she had about him. *Befriend him*, Chamberlain had said. She wondered just how different Adonis was now compared to how the viscount remembered him to be before whatever had happened that had changed him.

Something having to do with the war, no doubt. Some men came out of wars bolder and stronger, while others came out broken and beaten down. Adonis Truscott was apparently one of the broken ones.

Her pause in responding to his suggestion that they could do the ride another day was probably being misinterpreted by the man. "We shall do no such thing," she announced with a determined grin, deciding to make the best of it as she pulled on her kid gloves.

An obvious look of relief crossing his face, Adonis offered his arm and Lydia placed a hand on it. She couldn't help but notice how his height seemed to increase at least two inches when they took their leave of the townhouse and another six when he put on his top hat.

"Your hat is rather smart," Adonis murmured as they made their way down the two steps to the pavement. "Did you craft it yourself?"

Lydia resisted the urge to snort. "Thank you, but no. I saw it in the window of *Fitzsimmons and Smith* and simply had to have it."

"Ah, my favorite hat shop," the knight replied as he led her to her mount. "Hats that make the gentleman," he murmured after another moment, putting voice to the line that could be found embroidered into the label of every men's hat produced in the popular Oxford Street establishment.

"Mine, too," Lydia remarked as she approached her Welsh pony. "Except mine has a label that reads, "Hats that favor the lady.""

Holding the reins of both horses, the groom bowed at Lydia's approach. He was about to offer Sir Donald his horse and see to making a stirrup with his interlocked hands for Lydia when he was forced to take a step back. For Adonis had simply moved to stand in front of Lydia, placed his hands at her waist, and lifted her onto the side saddle.

Lydia couldn't help the sound of surprise she made just then, her hands instinctively moving to his shoulders as a means of hanging onto something as she was hoisted up. "Sir Donald!" she admonished him, although when she realized she was perfectly placed onto the saddle—she merely had to hook her right leg around the pommel and slide her left foot into the stirrup and she would be ready to ride—Lydia shook her head. "Really, sir, you must *warn* me before you go lifting me off the ground like that," she whispered.

Adonis furrowed his brows and blinked a couple of times. "I apologize, my lady. I merely thought it would be more expeditious this way. So your riding habit didn't have to be rearranged and all."

Taking a look at how the blue superfine of her skirt splayed evenly along the side of the pony, Lydia realized the man had a good point. The riding boot in the stirrup didn't even show beneath the edge of her hem. "Still, a bit of warning..." She stopped and heaved a sigh.

"A warning. I promise, my lady," Adonis stated with a nod. He turned and took the reins of his mount from the groom, giving the young man a wink before lifting himself into the saddle of his bay.

Lydia watched in fascination. Despite the man's need to use a cane—he definitely walked with a limp—he mounted his horse using his good leg and slid the cane into a leather sheath hung along one side of the horse. There was a moment when Lydia was sure he winced, though, and she thought perhaps riding caused him pain.

"Do you require a chaperone?" Adonis asked when Lydia seemed ready to leave. He glanced about as if he expected another horse to appear from behind the townhouse.

Lydia considered asking the groom to see about having a footman join them—or even the groom himself—but thought better of it. "Do I?" she replied with an arched eyebrow, rather liking how the knight seemed to visibly swallow just then.

So, he expected a chaperone, she realized. After the incident at the museum, she could understand why he might think she would prefer one. *Better to keep him guessing,* she decided.

"I shall see to your protection, of course," he stated, directing his horse into the street. "I am sworn to see to it, after all."

Lydia had her pony nearly abreast of his Cleveland Bay when she heard his claim. "Whatever do you mean by that?"

Adonis pretended not to hear her query. "Does her ladyship wish to join the parade in Rotten Row? Or would you prefer to ride somewhere else?"

Surprised by the offer of an option, Lydia considered where the 'somewhere else' might be. "Where did you have in mind, if not the park?"

The man allowed a shrug. "We could ride to the Serpentine," he suggested, thinking the poor weather would prevent too many people from being out by the water.

Rather surprised by the suggestion, Lydia figured it would be better to go somewhere they wouldn't be seen by the *ton.* She still wasn't sure about Adonis Truscott, so anything she could do to lessen unwanted gossip would help. "The Serpentine sounds divine," Lydia replied, digging her left heel into her horse as she leaned forward. Her pony was off at a fast trot, leaving behind a rather startled Adonis. His bay soon joined the Welsh pony, though, and together they dodged all manner of conveyances on their way west.

It wasn't until they reached the road just north of the Serpentine before the traffic thinned and it was quiet enough to make conversation.

Lydia turned her attention to Adonis and once again put voice to her query. "Whatever did you mean when you said you had promised my protection? You mentioned it last night, too." When the man didn't answer immediately, Lydia glanced in his direction and discovered his attention was on something far away. Following his line of sight, she couldn't make out what he seemed to find so interesting. "What is it?" she asked, pulling on the reins of her horse so that it stopped.

The Cleveland Bay took a few more steps before stopping, although Lydia could tell it did so of its own accord. The knight's attention was still on something else, and the only reason his horse had stopped was because her pony had halted so suddenly.

"Sir Donald!" she called out, tingeing her voice with urgency. Directing her mount to come abreast of the knight's, she was stunned to find the same blank look on Adonis' face as had been there the day before during the garden party. Reaching out with a gloved hand, she gave his shoulder a shake. "Sir Donald!" she repeated. When he still seemed lost in his thoughts, she nudged him again and said, "Adonis!" in a hoarse whisper.

The knight seemed to awaken from his stupor, his sudden gasp suggesting he hadn't taken a breath in a long time. His gaze darted about before it came to rest on Lydia. "How long?" he asked.

Lydia blinked before allowing a shrug. *How long?* "I've really no idea," she replied. "I just noticed you seemed... lost in thought."

"I apologize. I really have—"

"Where *were* you just then?"

The knight looked as if he wouldn't consider her question before he finally shook his head. "I really don't know that I was... anywhere," he replied, his brows furrowed. He looked as if he were concentrating, or at least trying to recall whatever it was that took him from the here and now.

"Then *when* were you?"

The question had Adonis turning his head quite suddenly. "When?" he repeated, his brows still furrowed. He struggled to remember what had him so mesmerized, so intent on the moment he became completely unaware of his surroundings.

"Yes. You must have been some *when* if not somewhere," Lydia reasoned.

The bay tossed its head, as if to signal its impatience. Adonis allowed the horse to walk, forcing the pony to step forward to keep abreast. The remnants of his waking dream —or was it a nightmare?—flitted about the edges of his vision. "A year ago, if you really must know," he murmured. *Smoke, the smell of gunpowder, a loud explosion and then... nothing but pain.*

Lydia seemed to think on his answer before asking her next. "Where were you a year ago?"

Adonis stiffened in the saddle. "I was in Hell, my lady," he murmured, almost too quiet to be heard.

When she thought he was about to get lost in his thoughts again, Lydia made to change the subject. "This is a bit of heaven, don't you think?" she asked as she waved a hand to indicate the beautiful green space around them. Despite the incessant rain and cooler temperatures, this area could boast a lawn of green and clear water near the bank of the Serpentine River.

Recognizing her ploy for what it was, Adonis dared a glance at their surroundings. He allowed a slight grin and nodded. But it wasn't the Serpentine or the beautiful green lawn that had him agreeing with her question, but rather her company, for he rather thought of Lydia as an angel just then. Wherever she was would always be just a bit of heaven, he decided. "Yes, yes indeed," he finally replied. "Would you care to walk for a time?"

Lydia gave the question some consideration before finally allowing a nod. She knew getting off her pony meant she would require a boost to get back on. Did the man simply wish to repeat what he had done earlier by lifting her onto the saddle?

Pulling his cane from its sheath, Adonis dismounted and pulled a carrot from his waistcoat pocket. His bay, more interested in the carrot than in any of the nearby vegetation, dutifully followed his owner as Adonis limped over to Lydia. She had already dismounted on her own, though, and regarded the odd gentleman with an arched brow. "I don't suppose you have another carrot stuffed into your pocket?" she ventured. Why, for a moment, she was quite sure Adonis was displaying the evidence of an arousal behind the placket of his riding breeches.

Adonis blinked. "I've only a lump of sugar, truth be told," he replied sadly as he pulled it from his pocket. He immediately offered it to her pony, who quickly saw it to its immediate demise before his own horse realized what had happened.

"Why, thank you, Sir Donald," Lydia spoke in a quiet voice, placing a hand on his arm even before he could offer it.

The knight seemed surprised by the move, although he recovered quickly and began leading them along the shoreline. Their horses followed behind, even though only Lydia held the reins to her mount. Fairly sure the Welsh pony would follow her, Lydia didn't want to risk his sudden departure. If he did decide to bolt, she would be forced to ride with Adonis on his mount.

Lydia decided the odd sensation she felt in response to that thought should be ignored just then.

"How is it you were at the garden party yesterday?" she asked after a few steps.

Adonis allowed a shrug. "I arrived uninvited, truth be told," he murmured, finally meeting her stunned gaze with a shrug. "You mentioned you would be there, and I wished to see you again," he said, rather matter-of-factly. "I am an acquaintance of both Lord Morganfield and Lord Torrington, of course," he added quickly, quite aware of Lydia's stunned expression.

"Are you always so bold?" she asked, hardly giving any credence to his claim that he attended the garden party only because he wished to see her. The man had a cheque for Lady Bostwick's charity in his coat pocket, the document already made out to the charity. Besides that, she hadn't mentioned anything about the garden party when she met the man in the museum.

I never mentioned the garden party because I hadn't yet received the invitation!

For a moment, Lydia wondered if she had lived an entire day and had no memory of it.

"Never, my lady!" Adonis responded, shaking his head, his face breaking out into a huge smile.

Lydia blinked. She was quite sure she had never seen a more beautiful man in her entire life. She was seeing the left side of his profile, of course, which meant his scarred cheek was hidden from view. But even the evidence of a bayonet wound did little to lessen his overall pleasing appearance. His dark blonde hair, far too wavy to work in the popular Titus style, was trimmed a bit long. Longer sideburns framed a face that probably wouldn't give away his age for many years to come. She had determined his eye color—brown—during the garden party, but she hadn't yet figured out his age.

"How is it you know of my knighthood?" Adonis asked, his arm stiffening beneath her hold. At Lydia's look of surprise, he added, "You've called me 'Sir Donald' several times today, which implies you know I was knighted."

Lydia wasn't about to tell him Lord Chamberlain had informed her, especially since he wasn't the first to say anything about it. "Lady Torrington mentioned it when she introduced us at the garden party yesterday," she responded with a grin. "I believe she learned of it from Lady Chamberlain. Actually, I wasn't positive it was you at first—I haven't been introduced to any men named 'Donald'."

Adonis seemed to think on her response for a time before allowing a nod. "She's a fine lady," he commented.

"Indeed. I often wonder how she and Lord Chamberlain ended up married—"

"She was a war widow, and he needed a wife. Her brother encouraged the marriage," Adonis stated quickly. "Not exactly a love match."

Lydia heard the hint of disapproval in his voice. She had heard Caroline Fitzsimmon's first marriage was to a military man—a man who had been killed in a battle before the two had been married even a month—and she wondered if that one had been a love match or simply a marriage of convenience.

The thought had her thinking on her own marriage. Why, she had barely known Jasper for a fortnight before he informed her they were to be married. As to whose convenience the marriage served, she could only guess that her father saw it as an opportunity to rid himself of a daughter past six-and-twenty. Jasper hadn't displayed any sign of affection during their brief courtship, but he had certainly been keen to her traits of noticing small details and her inquisitive nature.

She never expected to feel affection for the man who seemed so serious about his business. Secretive and yet friendly. He was good company if only because he was smart, and he could follow her line of reasoning whenever they discussed matters of importance.

"I know nothing about you, and yet I've allowed you to take me from my home to spend a rather cold and gray afternoon in your company," Lydia accused after a time, her head angling to one side. She was sure the man blushed at her words. "Why is that, exactly?"

Adonis once again seemed to grow a few inches taller with her words, his limp nearly disappearing as they walked. Another few steps, and his cane was resting over his shoulder.

"I am an agreeable sort," he replied lightly. "Given the right company."

Lydia allowed a mischievous grin. "I hardly know how it is you can believe I am good company. I have offended you, wounded you, aimed a gun at you—"

"Honored me, and humbled me," he broke in, finally daring a glance in her direction when he was aware she was staring. "Perhaps I'm of the opinion that any of your attention is preferred over none at all. There are probably others who are of the same opinion," he hinted, hoping she would tell him about the man who had paid a visit to her townhouse earlier that day. "Oliver Preston, perhaps?"

Gasping at his comment, Lydia nearly stopped in her tracks, but her pony seemed intent on keeping up with the larger Cleveland Bay. "Mr. Preston was a friend of my husband's. He... stops by on occasion to check on me, although he's to be married soon, so I rather doubt I will see him again," she explained, wondering what had Adonis mentioning the operative.

"Do you consider him... a friend?"

Taken aback by the question, Lydia angled her head. "Not particularly," she stated, remembering how ill at ease she had been in his company only a few hours ago. "What about you? Is he a friend of yours, perhaps?"

Adonis shook his head. "Perhaps at one time. A long time ago," he replied.

"Do you consider me a friend?" He had proposed the friendship yesterday, when they were about to drink their champagne.

Nearly stopping in his tracks, Adonis turned to stare at her. "Of course, milady," he stated, apparently stunned by the question.

"But, why?"

Blinking at her question, Adonis considered how to respond. "You're a rather lovely woman," he said finally. "Not at all what I expected."

Lydia blinked. *Expected?*

Well, this is rather unexpected, she considered. "How is it you had any expectations of me at all?" Lydia queried. A raindrop landed on her cheek, and she blinked before daring a glance up. "Oh, dear," she murmured.

Adonis was quicker in his response as he lifted her onto her pony. His hands continued to hold onto her waist as he stared up at her. "My apologies. I was supposed to warn you before I did that," he said.

Lydia blinked as she moved a gloved hand to cover one of his. "Apology accepted," she murmured, rather startled at how her body reacted to being held by him. *Jesus!* It hadn't been that long since a man had shown her any kind of attention, so why was she reacting so to Adonis Truscott?

The knight nodded and suddenly seemed conscious of where his hands were. He quickly pulled them away from her and retrieved his cane before mounting his bay in a practiced move. "Are you up for a race, my lady?" he shouted when a boom of thunder could be heard in the distance.

"Oh, if I must," Lydia replied with a sigh, rather disappointed the rain had begun to fall just as she was sure he was going to answer her question about how he had any expectations of her.

Using the riding crop to swat the right side of her pony, she kicked her left heel at the same time. The pony surged forward a few steps before she could get him turned around to come alongside Adonis and his mount, both horses easing into a gallop as they made their way back to town.

By the time they reached Bruton Street, Lydia's hat was soaked, but the superfine of her habit had shed most of the rain that pelted them.

"Come inside until the rain quits," she insisted as they pulled up in front of her townhouse. She issued the invitation even before she considered the ramifications. Her neighbors—at least those who had nothing better to do than to watch the traffic that passed by—would be well aware she was in the company of a gentleman. They would even pay witness to him entering her home, which probably meant a mention in the next issue of *The Tattler*.

Damn gossips, she thought.

Perhaps Adonis was aware of her immediate regret at having made the invitation, for he shook his head. "Thank you, my lady, but my sister is expecting me for dinner this evening," he replied as he dismounted. He was next to her horse in an instant, his limp having disappeared at some point during the afternoon. He reached up and, with his hands at her waist, he lowered her to the pavement just as the groom appeared from the mews behind the townhouse.

Lydia managed a curtsy and offered her hand when she noticed his raised brow. "Are you a wicked man, sir?" she asked in a quiet voice, wondering how he might respond. He was such an enigma, at once seeming to behave as an innocent when his actions suggested otherwise.

Adonis angled his head to one side and finally shook it. "I may have been at some point in my past, my lady," he said before lifting her gloved hand to his lips. "But I am no more." He bestowed a kiss on the back of her knuckles, completed his bow, and quickly remounted his horse. "Thank you for a rather pleasant afternoon. Despite the rain, I will do it again whenever you wish." He tipped his hat and then was off in the direction of Curzon Street.

Lydia watched as he made his way, wondering why he might ride in that direction just as the groom appeared to retrieve the pony. She gave him the reins and headed for the front door.

Lord Craven's residence is in Curzon Street, Lydia realized, remembering Adele's comment about his sister being Lady Craven.

Persephone Truscott.

Well, if their mother had nicknamed him 'Adonis', then it stood to reason she would have named her daughter after a Greek goddess. Too bad Persephone didn't seem happy with her lot in life, but then her oldest, Elizabeth, Lady Andrew, had died of pneumonia on the Continent. Lady Andrew's husband, Lord Andrew, was seeing to the three grandchildren with the help of a nanny somewhere near Geneva. Her two sons were away at school, leaving just Persephone with her husband, Robert Craven, Viscount Craven, in their townhouse.

Lydia had already determined there were no other Truscott family members—she had spent an hour the day before perusing her copy of *Debrett's* in search of information on Adonis—so she could understand Persephone's concern over her brother's behavior.

Given Lord Craven's reputation as a gambler, Lydia wondered if Persephone had married the viscount in an arranged marriage, or if perhaps she had been discovered in a compromising position and had been forced to marry him. Or perhaps she merely married him for what some said was a rather large fortune. She would no doubt outlive the man given his late nights spent in gaming hells.

Lydia shook the thoughts from her head, giving Jenkins a nod as she made her way into the vestibule. Her maid was already there with bath linens.

"Oh, you'll catch your death, my lady," Rachel murmured.

Wiping her face and the tops of her shoulders with the linen, Lydia shook her head. "I rather doubt a bit of rain will be my Waterloo," she murmured.

The word was out of her mouth before she had a chance to consider its importance.

Waterloo.

Her husband hadn't lived long enough to help in the defeat of Napoleon at Waterloo. Jasper had died two days before, somewhere near Ligny.

Reminded of how Adonis had acquired the scar on his cheekbone, Lydia thought perhaps Adonis had been in one of those battles. He had admitted to being on the Continent.

In Hell.

"Are you all right, my lady?"

Rachel's words had Lydia giving her head a shake. Goodness, if she wasn't careful, she would have her maid thinking she was a candidate for Bedlam. "Of course. I was merely woolgathering," she replied as she moved to make her way to the stairs.

"I cannot blame you, my lady. Given the cold and rain, we can use all the wool we can get."

Lydia managed a giggle as they made their way up to her bedchamber and a change into dry clothes, wondering the entire time when she might next find herself in the company of Sir Donald.

CHAPTER 15
DEDUCTIVE REASONING RETURNS

*M*eanwhile ...

Adonis paused his horse at the end of Bruton Street, half-tempted to turn back and beg for shelter from the rain. He gave a glance back to watch Lydia as she made her way into her townhouse, rather surprised at how his body reacted.

I've been too long without a woman, he reasoned at first, and then decided he was merely lying to himself. He had recognized his attraction to Lydia the moment he approached her in the museum. The moment he said the words that had him wincing and that immediately put her on the defensive.

I've been told I look exactly like him.

Or perhaps it was merely because he was standing so close to her. Close enough to sniff her perfume. Close enough to notice the soft curls at the back of her neck, and the whorl of her ear beneath her hat. Her perfect posture. Her elegance.

She wasn't supposed to be like this, he thought in dismay. He had imagined her a hag. Imagined her a prune-faced wretch. Imagined a shrew.

But she was none of those. Damn Jasper Barrymore. *Damn him all to hell!*

Well, he supposed his commander was already there. As

many times as he had remembered that afternoon and night on the battlefield, Adonis felt as if he were there, too.

This afternoon's outing had certainly changed his outlook, although something niggled at him. Made him wonder. Reminded him that he needed to study details, listen for tells, and watch for incongruities. If he had any hope of securing a real mission for the Foreign Office, he needed to prove he could still perform spy craft. It had been a year since his last mission, after all.

She lied to me.

Or did she?

Having spent the day watching her townhouse from a coach a few houses down from hers, Adonis knew Lydia hadn't paid any calls—she hadn't left the house the entire day —but someone had visited her.

This is most distressing, he considered as he allowed the Cleveland Bay to continue a slow walk, his thought of returning to her townhouse forgotten. He ignored the ever-increasing rain as he contemplated Lady Barrymore's answer to his query.

Why would she lie to me?

When he had asked her if Oliver Preston was a friend, she failed to mention the man had paid a visit to her just that afternoon. The man was due to marry in a few days. Why ever would he pay a call on Jasper Barrymore's widow unless they were friends?

He blinked, considering another alternative.

Lovers?

The thought nearly made him sick to his stomach. He had spent every night for four nights in her bedchamber, though, and on none of those occasions had she welcomed a visitor to her bed.

He shook his head, realizing he was allowing his imagination to get the better of him.

Tit for tat, I suppose, he considered then. He was sure she had caught his fib. The one where he claimed to have learned of the garden party from her. *Or did I simply imagine it so many times that I thought it was real?* Well, he was quite sure she realized she hadn't told him of the garden party—they hadn't been in one another's company for her to do so. He had merely read the invitation he had discovered on the hall table before he crept up to her bedchamber the night after they had met at the museum.

He hit himself upside the head, cursing when his gloved hand nearly crushed the brim of his dripping top hat. A shout from the driver of a dray cart brought him out of his reverie only to discover his horse had come to a complete stop in the middle of Green Street, not far from his bachelor quarters, but still out of sight of the mews and the stable hands who worked inside. Giving the bay a swift kick with a heel, he held on as his mount lurched forward.

Within minutes, a stableboy saw to his horse. "Are you aw' right, Mr. Truscott? Did he give you trouble?" the youth asked as he took the reins and offered the horse the stub of a carrot.

Adonis regarded the boy for a moment, wondering what had him asking. "No trouble," Adonis answered with a shake of his head, which sent a shower of water pouring from the brim of his hat. He remembered to fish a coin from his waistcoat pocket and toss it to the boy.

"Much obliged, Mr. Truscott," the stable hand said before he hurried off with the Cleveland Bay.

Nodding, Adonis made his way into his bachelor quarters, his manner most grim. When he caught sight of his reflection in the cheval mirror, his eyes widened.

No wonder the stableboy thought something was wrong, he realized. His drenched hat appeared crushed and misshapen, his face looked as if he had been crying, and his topcoat was splattered with mud.

"I'll draw a bath right for you straight away, sir," his batman announced from the threshold.

Adonis turned from the mirror and regarded Fitzroy for a moment, finally allowing a nod. "I'll be leaving again this evening, but I won't be joining my sister for dinner." The idea of spending time in Persephone's company rankled just then. *She thinks I'm a Bedlamite*, he remembered.

"Will you be going to your club then?"

Adonis blinked, thinking he should go somewhere for sustenance. He was in no mood for company, though. At least, not the company of men. A thought of paying a visit to a brothel didn't appeal just then either. His manner would probably frighten some poor lady of the evening and get him kicked out of the establishment. A gaming hell meant having to be civil to fellow gamblers, and he didn't think he could last the night before feeling the need to punch someone in the gut.

Or the face.

Despite what he had realized on his trip home, there was only one place he wanted to spend the night.

Lydia Barrymore's townhouse. Or rather, her bedchamber. He had a mission, and he intended to see it through to its end.

Whenever that might be.

"Nothing fancy, Fitzroy," he finally replied. "And have Cook make something I can take with me."

CHAPTER 16
A SUMMONS IS RECEIVED

*T*he following morning, June 20, 1816
Lydia had just reached the breakfast parlor when Jenkins intercepted her at the door. "This was just delivered, my lady," he said with an arched brow.

Examining the missive as she took it from the butler, Lydia realized why he seemed intrigued. "By a footman, I gather?" she replied, turning it over to examine the red wax seal on the back. Given its lack of any embossing, there wasn't a hint as to whom it was from.

Except she knew.

Lord Chamberlain.

"Yes, my lady."

"Is he waiting for a reply?"

The butler blinked, which only had Lydia feeling a hint of satisfaction. It was rare when something had Jenkins a bit discombobulated. "He is not. He left after making the delivery."

Lydia sighed. "Well, there's no hurry then," she said as she tucked the note into a pocket and made her way to her regular seat in the breakfast parlor.

One of the house's two footmen—there had been three, but without a husband in the household, the other one had left of his own accord to work for a neighbor—was quick to deliver a plate filled with coddled eggs, toast, and a slice of ham. One of the housemaids followed with a tea tray.

Once all the servants had left her alone, Lydia surreptitiously pulled the missive from her pocket and popped the seal.

Perhaps you thought your assignment was optional. It is not. Three o'clock, my office. C.

Lydia sighed, realizing from the tone of Lord Chamberlain's note that he was angry with her.

Or, mayhap just a bit impatient.

He probably didn't know about the ride she had taken with Sir Donald to the Serpentine. He certainly wouldn't know anything about the knight's nocturnal visits to her bedchamber. Although he wasn't in her bedchamber when she fell asleep, she had awoken to the sound of his soft snores. No longer alarmed by the thought of the man in her bedchamber, Lydia found she took comfort in his presence.

How odd. To have been so annoyed by Adonis Truscott only a few days ago, and now …

Well, now she had managed to annoy Lord Chamberlain.

Damnation!

Lydia considered how she might start her verbal report. *When I discovered Sir Donald had made himself at home in a Greek lounging chair in my bedchamber whilst I was sleeping, I promptly threatened him with my loaded pistol and demanded answers. He was most obliging.*

Except he wasn't.

Not really, anyway. He was keeping secrets from her, she was sure. Why, she didn't yet know.

After a moment, she decided it wasn't worth the attempt to shock the poor viscount. On second thought, she remembered Lord Chamberlain was beyond being shocked.

Well, she had some information to provide at least. Oliver Preston had paid a call, presumedly looking for Jasper's ring. She knew he wouldn't find it at the War Office —it was in the top tray of Jasper's jewelry box—which meant he would probably come back to the house to ask after it.

Perhaps it was fortuitous that Adonis Truscott had been paying visits to her bedchamber, after all. She at least knew some of what she was supposed to have learned about the man. She could rattle off the various facts and claim she was working on discovering more.

As for *when* that might be, she didn't exactly have another appointment set up with the man.

Would he show up in her bedchamber again tonight?

A shiver of something seemed to pass through her body just then.

Excitement? Anticipation?

She cursed to herself, annoyed that the man would have such an effect on her when she found him so... annoying.

As for the knight's sanity, she was quite sure he was merely misunderstood. His extended periods of staring at nothing at all were a bit problematic—and probably the reason his sister thought him a candidate for Bedlam—but she rather doubted it was a sign he wasn't in his right mind. If she could just figure out how to pull him back to the present—without having to yell his given name—and discover where he had been, Lydia thought it likely she could determine just why it was he spent so much time lost in thought.

When a footman reappeared to ask if she wanted anything else, Lydia was stunned to find she had eaten her entire breakfast. "I'd like another slice of ham," she murmured. "And coffee, if the cook has made any this morning."

The footman nodded. "She has, milady," he answered with a bow.

"Let Jenkins know I'll need the town coach at two o'clock."

"Yes, milady."

"And do be sure someone introduces you to Lady Pettigrew's lady's maid. She's really rather pretty and quite over the moon for you."

Lydia absolutely adored the way the footman's face

turned a brilliant red and his eyes widened in alarm. She thought for a moment if he might faint dead away, but the man quickly recovered his wits.

"Yes, milady," he said with a deep bow. With that, he took his leave of the breakfast parlor, his steps rather light.

Knowing she would be alone for only a few minutes, Lydia pulled the missive from her pocket and reread it. *Why did he give me this odd assignment?* she wondered for the tenth time. There were doctors better suited to determine just what ailed the knight.

Perhaps they had already been consulted. Perhaps they had employed leeches in an attempt to cure him. Given him arsenic or mercury or laudanum in an attempt to keep him in the here and now.

Lydia shivered at the possibilities of what might have been done to cure the man of whatever ailed him.

Poor Adonis, she thought, rather surprised at how she felt sorry for a man she had for the most part, until that moment, only found annoying.

Once the coffee and ham appeared before her, Lydia announced she would be in the study for the remainder of the morning, and she took her plate and cup with her as she took her leave of the breakfast parlor.

Downing her coffee with a grimace—*Good God, who had ever thought the beastly stuff worthy of drinking in the morning?*—Lydia pulled a parchment from a desk drawer and began recording everything she knew about Adonis Truscott.

CHAPTER 17
A VISIT TO WHITEHALL

Later that afternoon

At precisely one minute to three o'clock in the afternoon, Lydia Barrymore entered the open area outside the office of Lord Chamberlain, reported to his secretary, and took a seat in a rather uncomfortable chair meant for visitors to the viscount's office.

It was nearly four o'clock before she was called into Chamberlain's office. She was being punished, she knew, and decided not to complain.

"Lady Barrymore," Chamberlain said. He didn't get up from his chair, nor did Lydia expect him to.

"Lord Chamberlain. So good of you to summon me," Lydia replied in the most pleasant tone she could manage. She reached into her reticule and pulled out the parchment she had filled out whilst in the study earlier that day.

The viscount frowned when he realized she held more than one sheet. "And what's this?" he asked as he nodded toward the papers she held.

"Oh, this?" Lydia asked as she lifted the papers in a silk gloved hand. "It's what I've discovered about Sir Donald during our recent encounters. So far, at least. I expect I'll learn even more later tonight."

Matthew Fitzsimmons, Viscount Chamberlain, leaned

back in his chair and regarded the viscountess with an arched, bushy eyebrow. Although he tried hard, he couldn't hide the surprise he felt at hearing her words. "Let's have it then."

Lydia allowed a nod and began reciting everything she knew about Sir Donald. She never once looked at the papers she held, but she did put the front one behind the second page as she spoke, as if she had memorized every word and knew exactly where the notes continued onto the next page. "Have you any reports from doctors? Physicians?" she asked when she had completed her report. "That might assist me in this project?"

Lord Chamberlain sighed and pulled open a desk drawer. A thick stack of papers slammed onto his desk, the force of which had the other papers on his desk lifting up and moving slightly away from the offending pile.

Not bothering to hide her disappointment, Lydia allowed a sigh. "He is not insane," she murmured with a shake of her head. "Preoccupied, perhaps. Troubled, certainly. But he is not insane," she repeated.

The viscount nodded as he laced his fingers together. "These mostly have to do with his leg," he finally admitted. "Compound fracture, dressed in the field but not reset until he was in hospital in Brussels."

Lydia fought down the urge to wince. The man had to have been in severe pain for hours. Even more so when the bone was forced back into place. "He walks with a cane and usually limps a bit, but when he's doing something he enjoys..." She stopped, remembering how Sir Donald had been at the Serpentine, as if he had completely forgotten how to limp. "He walks quite normally," she finished after a moment. "Imagine that."

Lord Chamberlain frowned. "What was he enjoying?"

Despite her attempt to hide the embarrassment she felt just then, Lydia could feel a blush coloring her face. "Me, I suppose," she whispered. "Not in the way you're thinking," she quickly added with an arched brow. "It was as if he had completely forgotten where he was." She cursed herself for not having noticed it then. For not having made a conscious effort to determine exactly what they had been discussing when she noticed he wasn't limping. His cane had even been resting on his shoulder, as if he knew he wouldn't need it at all during their walk along the water's edge.

"Have you made arrangements for a liaison then?" Chamberlain asked, his eyebrow once again arched up. "At the theatre. In your private box, perhaps?"

Lydia stared at Lord Chamberlain, just then remembering the newest play at the Theatre Royal had already begun its run. *Damnation! How could I forget?*

"Not exactly," she said. She wondered if it might be too late to send the knight an invitation to join her. Where would she send it, though? Lord Craven's residence? Or Sir Donald's bachelor quarters? "But I suppose it could start there," she hedged.

The viscount actually seemed a bit surprised by her comment and then narrowed his eyes. "If not the theatre..." He blinked and didn't bother to finish the comment.

Lydia inwardly sighed. Did she really want to be seen in the man's company? She was sure there were already rumors about her and the knight, thanks to Lady Pettigrew. When the man was seen entering her box—and he would be seen— the rumors would only get worse. "But should I wish to have him join me, where might I send the request?" She avoided using the word 'invitation'. She didn't want Chamberlain thinking she *desired* the man's presence in her box.

"Why, I can pass it along, actually," the viscount replied lightly. "He's due to meet me here at five. He's of a mind to return to service, and despite your report, I still have my doubts as to his usefulness."

Lydia blinked, realizing she really had no say in the matter. "Then do so," she replied, making sure she lifted her head as she said the words. No need having the viscount thinking she was trying to avoid the knight. "If that's all..."

Lord Chamberlain angled his head. "I hope you're right,

Lydia. It's a shame what happened to him over there, but I want him to be right as rain," he whispered, as if he feared someone might be listening to their exchange.

"On an another note, I had a visit from Preston yesterday," she said carefully.

The viscount gave a start. "Social visit?"

"He tried to make it seem so, but he's looking for Jasper's ring," she replied. "I told him to check with the War Office, seeing as how I've never been given his personal effects."

Lord Chamberlain couldn't help but notice the bitterness in her voice. "Thank you for letting me know. It shan't be long now. I can't imagine he would leave Britain before completing that last assignment."

Angling her head to one side, Lydia asked, "Who gave him the assignment?" It had to be fairly recent. The man had been in her house several times during their *affaire*, and not once had he asked about the ring. Not once had he left her side to go searching in the master bedchamber, either. She had made sure the doors to that room were locked after Jasper's death—she didn't want anyone disturbing his things. Helping themselves to his bits of jewelry or trinkets or clothing.

Shaking his head, the viscount didn't reply right away. "Better you not know, but something tells me you already do."

So, Preston's latest assignment wasn't from this office, Lydia decided. That meant he probably was a double agent. Probably had been working for the French during those last days before the Battle of Waterloo. It was better that Jasper not know his friend was also an enemy.

Or perhaps he knew?

Giving the man a nod, Lydia stood up and gave a curtsy. "I do hope Lady Pettigrew will not be in attendance at the opening of the play," she murmured in a hint as she took her leave of Chamberlain's office.

The viscount allowed a sigh. He rather hoped not as well.

• • •

*A*s Lydia made her way back to her town coach, she had the niggling feeling she was being watched. Glancing about as if she were merely watching for traffic in Whitehall as she crossed the pavement to her town coach, she realized just why.

Adonis Truscott, wearing a cape coat and leaning heavily on his silver-topped cane, was watching her from in the front of his horse. Had followed her to the Foreign Office? If so, she hoped he hadn't been standing out in the cold the entire time.

Changing her steps so she headed in his direction, she gave him a brilliant smile. "Sir Donald!" she called out as she hurried up to him. She gave him a curtsy after he managed an awkward bow.

"Good afternoon, Lady Barrymore. I hope this day finds you well," he said as his eyes darted about. He took her gloved hand and kissed the back of it, obviously surprised at being discovered.

"It does indeed," she replied, "Now that I've found you," she said sweetly. "If you're not already occupied Saturday evening, perhaps you'll join me in my box at the Royal Theatre," she offered, realizing too late how awfully fast she sounded with the invitation. A reminder that he had been in her bedchamber until earlier that morning helped quell the thought, though.

The knight blinked twice before finally giving her a nod. "I appreciate the invitation, my lady," he managed with a nod. "I already have some place I must be later that evening, but I can certainly attend both engagements," he added with a wan smile and a half-bow.

Lydia regarded the beautiful man for perhaps a moment too long. "I look forward to it, then. I'm sure you know which box is mine. And if not, Lord Chamberlain can let you know when you meet with him at five o'clock. Don't be late. He's rather crotchety today," she said before bobbing a curtsy and heading back to her town coach.

Sir Donald watched as Lydia's driver held the door open for her, the man having already stepped down from the box when she first appeared from inside one of the Whitehall buildings.

Attending the theatre wasn't his favorite nocturnal activity, by any means, but Adonis found himself looking forward to a night spent in the company of Lady Barrymore. They would be in public, of course, but in a private box. And afterwards, in her bedchamber.

She wouldn't fall asleep at the theatre. At least, he didn't expect she would. As for later, he just hoped she wouldn't shoot him.

CHAPTER 18
A NIGHT OF DISCOVERY

uch later that night
The whisper of a kiss brought Lydia out of a deep sleep, one in which faces of familiar people swam by but no one seemed to recognize her.

Was a widow really so invisible? Forgotten by those who had been friends before her husband's death on the Continent?

Perhaps wearing widow's weeds really did render a woman forgettable.

Invisible.

Blinking away the last vestiges of the dream, Lydia drew in a quick breath and then another when she realized she wasn't alone. "Jasper?" she whispered, sitting up to glance about the dark room. The lamp on the nightstand had burned out at some point, and the embers of the last lumps of coal were barely glowing in the fireplace.

The scent of sandalwood lingered in the chilly air, and she realized almost immediately it wasn't because Jasper was in the room.

Jasper was dead. Run through by a bayonet somewhere near Brussels. Somewhere on the road between Charleroi and Brussels.

A year ago.

The familiar sensation of her chest compressing, of tears about to spill forth, had her swallowing.

Hard.

"Should I be?"

The hoarse whisper had her gasping. The voice wasn't Jasper's, but it was definitely male. Familiar.

"Sir Donald?" she replied, disbelief evident in her voice. She turned to her right and realized the knight was standing at the edge of the bed, his silhouette apparent because his white shirt appeared almost ghostly in the inky blackness. If he had been wearing a waistcoat and topcoat when he arrived, he wasn't now.

"What are you doing here? How... how did you get in this time?" she asked in an urgent whisper, sure the lock on the back door had been repaired that day.

Or had it?

Lydia had a mind to threaten him again with the gun she kept beneath the pillow next to hers, but thought it a bit late to be pulling it on him now. She considered claiming she would scream if he didn't take his leave immediately, but the thought of how the servants would gossip—who would believe she hadn't invited the man for a liaison?—had her resisting the urge.

When the edge of the mattress depressed, Lydia knew he was sitting next to where she sat. As her eyes finally adjusted to the darkness, she was able to make out his face.

"The lock on the back door is still broken," he replied quietly. "And it is exactly because of it that I am here."

When she realized how close he was, Lydia clutched the bed covers to her neck. Goodness! She could reach out and touch him!

"I made a promise, you see. I am here to keep that promise."

The words were familiar. Or perhaps it was merely the sentiment, for he had intimidated he was to provide protection for her when he had come to fetch her for the ride the day before. "You will tell me once and for all, to whom did you make such a promise?" she asked, not bothering to whisper just then. Her voice sounded loud in her ears, though. Beneath the covers, she pulled her knees up and wrapped her arms around them. Tucked into a ball, she felt safer given how close Adonis was. Why, he was so close, she could feel heat emanating from his body! "And why?"

For a moment, she wondered why she hadn't simply begun screaming at the top of her lungs when she realized he was in her room.

A man was in her bedchamber.

A man she barely knew, and yet, he obviously meant no harm.

And had no intention of bedding her.

The last thought had her feeling a hint of disappointment before she remembered how he shouldn't even be *in* her bedchamber.

What is wrong with me?

*A*donis regarded her for a time, rather pleased to find she wasn't wearing a white mob cap with her virginal white nightrail. The lace and lawn ruffle decorating the neckline had him wondering what she might look like in a ballgown. What she might look like in nothing at all. "My commanding officer," he replied, struggling to fight the sudden arousal he felt at being in her company.

He hadn't expected to feel an attraction to the widow. Indeed, he had thought his duty to keep his promise would be tedious. Trying. But the afternoon ride and the walk along the Serpentine had been rather pleasant. He could understand how it was Jasper Barrymore felt affection for his wife.

I never said the words.

"He was near death and knew it. He... he wanted to ensure your safety. He... he had regrets," he stammered before allowing a sigh of frustration.

Lydia sucked in a breath. He was speaking of Jasper. He had to be. But how? How could he know her husband?

Jasper had been an officer in the British Army, but until the year prior, he had never left Britain. Never fought against Napoleon's forces. Probably never shot a man nor used his sword to draw blood.

Spy craft rarely requires violence, he claimed when he first admitted he wasn't a typical English army officer. *I report to the War Office and, when the occasion requires it, to the Foreign Office,* he had explained shortly after they said their marriage vows in front of a vicar in the small church in Kent. He had spoken the words in a whisper whilst he held her the first night of their marriage. The first night she realized she had married a man she barely knew in exchange for his protection.

What had compelled Jasper Barrymore to marry her in the first place, though?

They hadn't courted in the usual sense. Jasper simply appeared at Parkhurst House in Wickham and asked for an introduction—they had only shared a dance at Lord Huntington's ball—his reason being a recommendation from a friend who knew of her status as an unmarried daughter of Harold Grandby. A few visits later, he presented her with a simple gold band and requested her hand in marriage.

Her father claimed no foreknowledge. Her much older brother, William, claimed never to have met the man. Although she found the officer's company pleasant enough, she was more surprised than anyone that he proposed marriage given her dowry wasn't as much as it should have been for a daughter of a viscount. Her father had never been good managing his funds, and she rather doubted her brother was any better now that he had inherited the viscountcy.

On the morning of their wedding, Lydia finally broached the subject, thinking she would give the man an out should he have changed his mind about wanting to marry her. The last thing she wanted was to marry a man who didn't wish to be her husband.

Remember, it was I who sought out you, Jasper had replied

as he bestowed a kiss on the back of her hand. He turned her hand over then and placed a kiss in the middle of her palm, allowing his lips to linger before he finally straightened. *Mayhap, have you changed your mind?*

Blinking at the sensation his lips had created in the palm of her hand, Lydia had simply given her head a quick shake. *I have not*, she had replied. *Indeed, I look forward to being your wife.*

They were wed a half-hour later. After a fortnight of marriage, Jasper took his leave of her for nearly a week, explaining he had business in Newmarket. When he returned, he announced they would be living in a townhouse in London. *My work requires my presence there*, he explained. *I do hope you won't miss your family too much.*

Truth be told, she didn't miss her father or her brother at all. Excited for the opportunity to live in the capital, Lydia had packed everything she owned, joined her husband in a rented carriage, and made the move from Kent the following week. It was then she learned how little she knew of her husband's profession, for the man was rarely home for dinner and left London for weeks at a time. It was during one of those extended absences when Lord Chamberlain requested she pay a visit to Whitehall.

His proposition had seemed preposterous. And yet, she had agreed without a second thought.

Read the reports from operatives who spy for your King and country, Chamberlain had said, one of his bushy eyebrows arched up. *After you've decoded them. Provide analysis. Are you interested?*

Of course she was interested. It was a way to fill the boring days waiting for Jasper's return from wherever duty took him.

When Jasper was home, she resumed her life as a viscountess, hosting parties and playing wife to a man who seemed to adore her more each time he returned. *Absence makes the heart grow fonder*, he had murmured one night after a spirited night of lovemaking.

Lydia thought she had never heard more welcome words. She learned to appreciate the time they did have together, joining Jasper in his bed on the nights he didn't pay a visit to hers. And then Jasper announced he would be leaving for the Continent for a campaign against Napoleon.

Three weeks later, he was gone.

She never saw him again, although she received letters from him every few days, their crumpled state a testament to the distance they had traveled to reach her. And probably to those who had read them as they made their way to England.

The fourth letter had her finally understanding just why he was on the Continent. The revelation had been somewhat profound. *My horse is a magnificent bay*, he wrote in that letter. *Proud and powerful, with a mane that reminds me of your beautiful mahogany hair.*

Mounted on that war horse, he had probably seemed rather larger than life. Lydia could just imagine him, sword raised in the air, his other hand holding the reins of his black horse as it reared. As for the mention of her hair, she thought he would be shocked at seeing how gray it had become in the past year.

I shall do what I must to see that the emperor is dethroned and that France can no longer wage war on its neighbors. This has become my newest mission, one in which my closest associates are involved. I am determined we shall prevail.

Lydia shook her head, aware that Adonis was regarding her with what she could barely make out as an arched eyebrow.

"I loved him," she stated, a sob threatening to rob her of breath. "I would not have married him had I not felt at least a bit of affection for him. It was I who was never sure if the feeling was reciprocated." She swallowed and struggled for a breath. "Jasper wasn't one to speak of such things..."

Absence makes the heart grow fonder.

Her hand was suddenly covered with another, the larger hand's warmth permeating her skin in an instant. She gave a start and raised her eyes to meet those of Adonis.

"He did, though. I assure you," Adonis said in a quiet voice.

Lydia shook her head. "Had he truly loved me, he wouldn't have left me behind at every turn of his career," she whispered hoarsely, struggling to fight another sob. She wouldn't cry. She was done crying over Jasper Barrymore.

"If you were a man, I would strike you for saying that," Adonis claimed in a clipped voice.

Lydia inhaled, visibly recoiling at hearing his harsh words, at sensing how his hand tightened atop hers. "For speaking the truth?" she countered, daring him to do his worst.

Adonis' eyes darkened as he angled his head. *To whose truth was she referring?* How could it be any other way but how he remembered it?

"Viscount Barrymore's only regret before he died was that he couldn't be with you. To tell you of his affection. Of his regret that he never got a child on you," Adonis countered in a harsh whisper. He paused a moment. "He thought you would make a wonderful mother."

Lydia couldn't help how her body jerked in response to the words. A sense of overwhelming guilt gripped her. It was true she had never been with child. She simply thought herself barren, despite her monthly courses. "He was so rarely in residence," she murmured. "I would have gladly borne his child," she added in a whisper, her burst of anger having passed as quickly as it had come.

Before she was quite aware of what was happening—when had the tears begun to fall?—she felt his arms wrap around her shoulders, felt herself being pulled so her head fell against his chest. Felt his chin rest on her head as he murmured something comforting. Something reassuring.

Within moments, she fell asleep, her body finally settling against the front of his.

• • •

*A*donis slept soundly for the first time in over a year, his last thoughts of Lydia's first word when she realized there was someone in her bedchamber.

Jasper.

That her late husband's name would come to her lips before words of fright or suspicion had him so surprised, he couldn't help the feeling of relief that washed over him. He had spent an entire year imagining what she might be like, at least on the few days he had the full use of his faculties and wasn't losing entire hours spending too much time in his head.

He imagined her cold-hearted. Warm-hearted. Cruel. Kind. Demanding. Easygoing. Ugly. Gorgeous. Large. Small. Round. Tall. Short.

He never imagined her to be what she was—a complex, beautiful, wounded woman who had no idea how it was she ended up married to the likes of Jasper Barrymore.

Perhaps she didn't want to know. At least she knew Jasper Barrymore was a spy. How many wives of spies could admit to knowing their husband's profession?

How many spies are even married?

A year ago, Commander Jasper Barrymore, bleeding profusely and struggling to catch his breath, had professed to love his wife. To feel regret at having left her in London whilst he led a small contingent of Wellington's men to what would be their almost total demise. "I never spoke the words, nor did she, but I go to my death hoping... *believing* she loved me," he struggled to get out as Adonis tried to make him comfortable on the ground of the battlefield on which most of their small band of soldiers had perished.

The words.

Men are such fools, Adonis remembered thinking that day, and again later that evening as the smoke cleared and the evidence of a battle lost made itself completely apparent. The impact of what he had promised his commander hit him harder than the Frenchman who had attempted to kill him. The one he had dispatched with a single bullet to the head.

"Promise me you'll look after her," Jasper whispered, his gasps for air more labored now that he seemed to be choking on his own blood.

"I will, of course," Adonis had replied, his words meant more to placate than to promise.

"Provide protection," Jasper Barrymore ordered. The commanding officer coughed several times, the spasms becoming weaker as he bled out. "Promise me, Truscott. There's a knighthood in your future, you must know."

Adonis remembered thinking he didn't give a rat's ass if there was a knighthood scheduled to be bestowed on him. The pain in his leg was so severe, he was sure he would pass out at any moment, probably die from his wound.

Making the promise had been easy, for at the time, he didn't think he would live to see the next day, let alone the shores of Britain.

To see her.

"I will, I promise," he repeated, hoping his words would allow the commander to simply give up and die properly.

But, then, Adonis didn't die as he should have. Anyone who paid witness to his wounded leg would think he should have perished the moment it broke. Seeing part of a bone jutting out from beneath the skin should have made him physically ill, but he was so spent—so exhausted—he couldn't muster the necessary response. It was as if he was seeing someone else's fractured leg. Someone else's limb stretched out in front of him.

His commander, leaning heavily against his left side, wasn't aware of the blood that dripped down Adonis' right cheek, making it appear as if he cried tears of blood.

The commander finally took his last breath just as the sun appeared on the eastern horizon. A few minutes later, another group from Wellington's contingent—those left from the battle closer to Brussels, found Adonis and loaded him onto a stretcher. The pain had been so excruciating, he found he had to retreat into his head to tolerate the agony. He remembered a Dutch doctor saying he would be taking the leg, while another argued it could be saved. Another round of agony, another visit to the inside of his head and pleasant thoughts that helped him keep what little sanity he had left.

Was it any wonder he still preferred to retreat into his head when he sensed the need for safety? When he needed a blissful state of existence without pain?

So why did he tend to revisit that afternoon on the battlefield? That night? The following morning?

Or the week before? When he had discovered the lifeless body of the only woman he had ever loved?

For when his thoughts took him from the here and now, they tended to drift to a time when he felt exhaustion, pain, despair, hunger, and thirst. To a time of his greatest loss. To a time when he held up Jasper Barrymore during his last hours.

Was the weight of a promise made to a dying man really so crushing?

Now that he'd had a chance to converse with Lady Barrymore, Adonis wondered if Jasper Barrymore had known exactly what he was doing. By making Adonis promise to provide protection for his widow, Lord Barrymore was ensuring Adonis would be forced to meet her. Spend time in her company. Stay with her every night.

Did the man also know Adonis would come to feel affection for her? For what else could explain why it was he felt compelled to kiss her the very first moment he was alone in her company?

But what had compelled her to kiss him?

Adonis hugged Lydia closer and finally settled her onto the bed. For the first time in a year, Adonis found himself thanking instead of cursing Jasper Barrymore.

"Go to sleep, my lady," he murmured.

But Lydia Barrymore was already sound asleep.

CHAPTER 19
A PUZZLE PROVES PUZZLING

The next morning, June 21, 1816

Despite having cried herself to sleep the night before, Lydia awoke feeling rather refreshed, a feeling of calm having settled over her at some point during the night.

Perhaps it was because a year had passed since Jasper's death and it was time to move on with her life. Her year of mourning was over, even though she would be considered a widow for the rest of her life. Or perhaps it was because she'd learned more about Jasper's fate. About his last hours of life.

Yes, that was it, she decided. Just knowing how he died provided some closure. Knowing he was in the company of Adonis Truscott certainly explained why the knight felt compelled to spend time in her company—far better it was someone she now knew than some stranger she could never hope to meet.

Rachel opened the drapes and was about to head to the fireplace when she realized her mistress was awake. Lydia had already started pulling on the wool stockings the maid had left on the edge of the bed.

"Good mornin', milady," Rachel said as she bobbed a curtsy. "I'm to tell you a footman just delivered a new puzzle. Jenkins put it in the parlor," she added as she picked up the empty coal can from the hearth. "I'll be back to help you dress," she said, turning to leave the bedchamber as Lydia frowned.

A puzzle? *But I haven't ordered one*, she thought before she realized from just where the footman might have come. She had her chemise and wool stockings pulled on before Rachel returned with the coal. "No need to start another fire," she said as the maid set the coal bucket on the brick hearth. "I'll be heading down to the parlor just as soon as I'm dressed."

Rachel blinked. "So, will you be taking your breakfast in the parlor then, milady?" she asked as she set a cup of chocolate on the dressing table.

"Yes, that will do," Lydia replied, not having thought about breakfast since Rachel's news of the delivery. She set about getting into a corset while the maid helped with the ties. "Has there been any word from the locksmith?"

There was a pause as Rachel pulled the corset strings tight and hurriedly laced them. "Jenkins says the man is due this mornin'. Not a moment too soon, if ya ask me, seein' as how someone was in the gardens last night."

Lydia stiffened, as much from the tightening of the corset as from hearing Rachel's words. "Someone?" she repeated as she nearly turned around.

Rachel nodded. "Some street urchin, Elsie says. The boy was helpin' himself to a carrot, even though they is barely an inch long."

The relief Lydia felt at hearing it was merely a boy was palpable. "Surely the household can spare a carrot. The poor boy must have been starving," she replied, her hands resting on her hips as Rachel finished with the corset and started to tie the petticoat she had pulled on.

Elsie, the kitchen maid, probably didn't see it that way, but then she had been a starving urchin when she was discovered stealing by the next door neighbor. Lydia had been quick to take responsibility for the girl before a parish constable could be summoned.

"Still, he was *stealin'*, milady," the maid responded in disgust.

Lydia wondered how her maid could begrudge a starving boy a carrot, but decided to let the matter drop. As long as Adonis Truscott hadn't been discovered in her garden—or anywhere else on her property—she was fine.

Once she was dressed, Lydia hurried to the parlor, her cup of chocolate in hand. The paper-wrapped box gave no indication as to its origin nor who might have sent it. She studied the white string that kept the folded paper in place, the precise diagonal folds at the corners suggesting it had been meticulously wrapped. Peeking into the folds at one end revealed a note tucked therein.

Lydia grinned as she carefully pulled it out and opened it. Folded just once, the small, bright white parchment revealed only a few words. *In preparation for your next assignment. C. Postscriptum. Ask for help from your current assignment. That's an order.*

Straightening on the settee, Lydia frowned. *Damn him!* Lord Chamberlain meant for her to solve the puzzle with Adonis present. She had a half a mind to send the box back to the Foreign Office—or even deliver it herself—but a combination of curiosity and intrigue gripped her as she slowly undid the string tie and carefully unwrapped the paper.

Removing the pasteboard lid, she stared down into a box containing hundreds of tiny, thin pieces of mahogany, some displaying odd marks on one side while the other sides were left blank. She was about to spread them out on the low table and realized she really shouldn't leave the pieces out for any of the servants to see.

Glancing at the card table farther back in the room—it sported the dissected geographical map of Europe she had finished a few days ago—she decided to simply scoop those pieces back into their box and use the table for this one.

Jenkins appeared with her breakfast as she finished

clearing the table, his rather stunned expression giving away his shock at seeing the map completely dismantled.

"I'll eat here," Lydia announced as she set aside the old puzzle and placed the new box on top.

"Very well, my lady," he murmured as he arranged the tray on the table and removed the silver lid from a plate containing coddled eggs, toast and a slice of ham. Another cup of chocolate completed the breakfast. "I'll see to a fire right away."

Lydia glanced at the clock over the fireplace mantel. "If I'm still here at noon, do interrupt me, won't you? I have to pay calls this afternoon," she ordered as she dumped the box of tiny pieces onto the tabletop.

The butler blinked at the assortment of puzzle pieces that spilled forth, the pyramid slowly flattening as the pieces spread out. "Very good, my lady." He moved to the fireplace, lit a few pieces of tinder with a flint, and took his leave of the parlor.

An hour later, half her breakfast forgotten and all the pieces turned so their marked sides lay facing up, Lydia shook her head. *This makes no sense*, she thought as she studied what she had come to believe was tiny writing. She thought the pieces might be a runes—ancient symbols from an old version of the German alphabet—but their shapes were all wrong. Some lined up and seemed to fit together, although she couldn't be sure they were in the right order. Curved and straight edges lined up, but with dozens of pieces cut in the exact same shape, she realized she would have to study the lines more closely to determine just exactly where each one would fit.

When Jenkins showed up at precisely noon, Lydia stared at him and then at the mantel clock in surprise. She had barely made any progress, sure there must either be some pieces missing or far more than were necessary to complete whatever it was she was supposed to decode. Reminded of the note that Lord Chamberlain had included, she felt a hint of annoyance. What could Adonis Truscott know that would help solve the puzzle?

"Have Rachel meet me upstairs. I need to change to make calls. And please don't allow anyone to touch anything," she said as she motioned to the tabletop.

"Very good, my lady," Jenkins murmured, removing the breakfast tray as he took his leave.

With another glance at the pieces before she, too, took her leave, Lydia did a double-take. She stepped out of her slippers and climbed atop the chair in which she had been sitting, careful to balance herself as she held up her skirts. From the higher vantage point, she realized the markings on the pieces were probably part of a large drawing. She couldn't yet tell what the drawing was supposed to depict, but when she returned to the project later that day, she could at least concentrate on completing a drawing instead of trying to spell out words or codes.

I'll be damned if I ask for help from Sir Donald, she thought as she made her way upstairs. *That's an order, indeed.*

CHAPTER 20
PAYING CALLS

Two o'clock in the afternoon
If a lady called upon another and found she wasn't in residence, it was usually because that lady was paying a call on someone else. Since some ladies paid their calls in the late mornings, some chose to pay their calls in the afternoons. Knowing which ladies stayed at home and which ladies paid calls in the afternoons gave Lydia an advantage. By going to Worthington House, she could be sure to find a number of ladies in the company of Adele Slater Worthington Grandby, Countess of Torrington.

"I cannot tell you how happy I was to see you at the garden party," Caroline Fitzsimmons, Viscountess Chamberlain, said as Lydia joined a group of women in the parlor. The tea tray had just been delivered, and Adele was doing the honors.

"I was so happy to be there," Lydia replied, nodding to the other ladies in attendance as she took a seat. "I do hope Lady Morganfield collected enough donations." Had the marchioness had made mention of Sir Donald's contribution to her favorite charity?

"She did fine, as she always does," Clarinda Fitzwilliam, Countess of Norwick, stated with a grin. "I think Morganfield secretly adds money to the pot when she's not looking," she added, referring to Adeline Carlington's husband, the Marquess of Morganfield.

There was a round of titters before Adele passed out cups and saucers. "Lady Morganfield was very pleased, in fact. One particular gentleman was apparently quite generous." Her gaze went to Lydia as she made the comment.

Her teacup halfway to her lips, Lydia was aware of several pairs of eyes aimed in her direction. "You must be referring to Sir Donald," she said quickly, hoping someone would change the subject.

"Sir Donald?" another piped up. "Who is that?"

One after another of the women offered what they knew of the man, the collective knowledge finally ending with a comment about how Lady Craven thought her brother a Bedlamite.

Lydia inwardly sighed. Despite his frequent episodes of staring at seemingly nothing at all, she didn't think the man insane. He just seemed... preoccupied. A deep thinker, perhaps.

Troubled maybe. How could he not be? The man had paid witness to one of the worst battles of the war, and nearly lost his leg as a result.

He watched Jasper die.

"Have you paid witness to his bouts?"

Startled by the question—especially when she realized it was directed to her—Lydia shook her head. "Not that I'm aware," she lied, not sure what else to say. She wasn't about to tell them about the incident at the Serpentine, or about what had happened during the garden party. "He seemed completely in the moment when I spoke with him in the gardens at Carlington House a few days ago."

A few women were murmuring about something unrelated when Lady Pettigrew leaned in her direction. "Did you enjoy your ride with the gentleman?"

Lydia stiffened in her seat, well aware of how the conversation in the parlor seemed to cease all at once as everyone stared in her direction. "It was quite pleasant. At least, until it started to rain. I don't believe I've ever managed such a quick ride back to my townhouse as I did that day," she said with a forced grin.

"Has Mr. Truscott been a frequent caller during your mourning period?"

Lydia was quite sure she heard Adele gasp at Lady Pettigrew's query. "Not at all. Actually, I didn't have the pleasure of meeting Sir Donald until Lady Morganfield's garden party," Lydia replied.

Lady Pettigrew could barely hide her surprise at hearing Lydia's reply. "I would have thought from how he lifted you onto your horse that you two were... *intimate*," she countered.

Pasting a smile onto her face, Lydia considered how she should respond. She had considered that someone might have paid witness to the knight's inappropriate move the day of their ride; she should have known someone in the neighborhood would pass along the news to someone like Lady Pettigrew. Angling her head to one side, Lydia replied, "Goodness, no. I just lacked a mounting block, and given Sir Donald's injured leg, it was far easier for him to lift me up than to bend down and form a stirrup with his hands," she replied in a voice loud enough to be heard by everyone. "He is *such* a gentleman."

Murmurs of agreement made the rounds of the room while Lady Pettigrew realized her gossip didn't have the profound effect she was hoping to achieve. Adele, bless her heart, brought up the discussion of the next ball.

With the attention off of her, Lydia was able to drink her tea before it cooled off too much. It was when there was just a few teaspoons left in the bottom when she noticed the arrangement of tea leaves. She was reminded of the puzzle pieces and the image they might form.

Why would Lord Chamberlain insist Sir Donald be included—nay, be required—to help solve the puzzle?

"Sometimes our men just have to be included in what we're doing," Clarinda was saying. "Norwick can become so grumpy when he feels left out, even when he claims he wants to be."

Lydia blinked.

Was that what this was about? Chamberlain deciding Sir Donald had to be included in something so that he wouldn't feel left out? Did the director think the newly minted knight's bouts of staring at nothing could be cured by giving the man something to do? Something to occupy his time?

His mind?

She supposed that had been Lord Chamberlain's reason for sending the puzzle. And including the order that Sir Donald be included in helping find the solution.

Why hadn't he just sent it to the knight directly? But then the missive attached might have included the instruction for *her* to be included in solving the puzzle.

The meddling man.

Sighing, Lydia realized she would have to send word to Adonis Truscott to join her at the townhouse. Just the thought had her wondering how he might arrive without being seen by the neighbors ...

She blinked. And blinked again.

He had arrived last night and left this morning without being seen. He had, in fact, done it several times! He implied it wouldn't be his last visit since he was sworn to... what had he said?

Provide protection.

Well, if the man showed up in her bedchamber tonight, she would be taking him to the parlor. They would have to work on the puzzle by the light of a candle lamp, but at least it would give the man something to do. Something to keep him in the here-and-now.

Something to keep her sane.

CHAPTER 21
A SOLUTION BEGETS
ANOTHER PUZZLE

ater that night
The sound of the back door opening had Lydia stiffening. She stood just inside the kitchen, waiting on a teakettle that was about to begin whistling in protest. Grabbing a towel from the nearby counter, she quickly removed the kettle from the stove's hot surface and poured the contents into a teapot.

"I wondered when you might arrive," she said in a hoarse whisper. Despite the locksmith having been at the house earlier that day, she was sure it was Adonis Truscott who managed to gain entrance through the back door.

Damn him and his stubbornness.

She glanced around the edge of the door jamb, almost relieved to find Adonis staring at her in alarm. "I see hiring a locksmith wasn't of any use. I do hope you didn't damage the new lock whilst breaking in."

"Why are you still up, my lady?" the intruder asked in a hoarse whisper, the evidence of his surprise at finding her in the kitchen still on his face. He surreptitiously slid a lock pick set into his pocket, tucking his sketchpad beneath his other arm as he did so.

"We have an assignment," she countered as she finished

setting up the tea tray. "Do you require anything stronger than tea for the night?"

Adonis silently moved into the kitchen, his eyes widening as he took in the sight of the midnight repast Lydia had assembled. A tray of smoked meats and cheeses was decorated with cut fruits. The tea tray included the usual cups and saucers along with a plate of biscuits and several slices of cake. "Are you expecting... someone?"

Lydia gave him a quelling glance. "No one besides you," she answered as she lifted the tray of meats and handed it to him.

Adonis blinked, but took the tray, gripping his sketchpad beneath his elbow. "I don't expect you to *feed* me, my lady," he murmured, although his mouth watered at the thought of helping himself to some of what was on the tray he held.

"Nonsense. You'll feed yourself. We have work to do, and it may take all night," she countered as she lifted the tea tray. When Adonis didn't move from where he stood, she sighed. "To the parlor," she ordered. "We have a puzzle to solve."

The knight's eyes widened at her comment. "From Chamberlain?" he queried.

Lydia nodded as she led the way to the parlor, her slippered feet making no sound on the marble tiled floor of the grand hall. She considered how the knight knew Chamberlain had sent the puzzle. *Had he received a missive with instructions as well?*

Adonis' boots were barely audible as he made his way from the kitchens to the grand hall. The light of a candle lamp on the tea tray illuminated their path as they made their way, even though a few gas-fed sconces on the hall walls were lit.

Once inside the parlor, Lydia shut the door and led them to the card table where the puzzle pieces were as she had left them earlier that day. She set the tea tray on an adjacent table, one she had instructed Jenkins to add before she left to pay calls earlier that afternoon.

Adonis stared down at the puzzle pieces spread out on the card table. "Oh, my," he murmured in a whisper.

Lydia took the tray of meats and cheeses from him. "Do you require any fortification in your tea, Sir Donald?" she whispered as she poured a cup of tea.

Settling into the chair on the opposite side of the table from Lydia, Adonis shook his head. "Pretend that I have no idea of what is about to transpire, and form your response accordingly. What is this about?" He waved a hand over the card table and included the trays of tea and sustenance as he set his sketchpad so it leaned against the table leg.

Sighing, Lydia crossed her arms over her middle. "Didn't you receive a missive from Lord Chamberlain with instructions to solve a puzzle with me?" she asked, not hiding her annoyance. She reached down and plucked the viscount's note from under the pasteboard box the puzzle pieces had been in. Handing it over to Adonis, she gave him an arched eyebrow. The brighter lighting in the parlor allowed her to see him. Wearing no cravat or waistcoat, he looked as if he could have passed for a crew member on a pirate's ship. His shirt was black—probably bombazine, Lydia thought, the familiar fabric a staple in her wardrobe for the past year. Black breeches, but not those worn for formal occasions, and black boots sans any tassels or other decoration, completed his outfit. She realized the clothes were utilitarian, good for wearing when one didn't wish to be noticed at night. When one needed to hide in the shadows. *A highwayman!*

No wonder the man hadn't been seen entering or leaving her house.

Adonis read the note by the light of the candle lamp, his brows furrowing as he did so. "I'm of a mind to challenge him to a duel," he murmured as he raised his eyes to regard Lydia. "Rather... cheeky of him, don't you suppose? Not to mention, a bit on the improper side?"

Lydia angled her head to one side. "As you have probably already surmised, I have worked for Lord Chamberlain in the past. Lord Barrymore..." She pause, realizing she might be admitting too much by mentioning her husband had arranged the assignment. *Probably before he even married me,* she thought when she remembered Chamberlain's edict to see to Adonis' sanity.

Marry him if you have to.

"Lord Barrymore arranged for my employment at the Foreign Office after we wed. Now that my mourning period is over, I wish to return to service. I'll do whatever I must to gain a suitable assignment, preferably one in which I can remain in London and review reports from overseas operatives. It's what I used to do during the war," she explained in a low voice. "It's either that, or I'll need to seek employment with *The Times.*"

Adonis stared at her, his mouth slightly open as she made her declaration. "Whatever you *must?*" he repeated in a whisper, a look of hurt crossing his too-handsome face. "Does that mean—?"

"Whatever I must," Lydia repeated. "Now, if you do not wish to find yourself married because of a scandal, I suggest you help me solve this puzzle and see to leaving this house before my rather nosey neighbors pay witness to your presence," she added with an arched eyebrow. "Lady Pettigrew already knows you lifted me onto my pony the other day."

The knight regarded her for a moment, rather stunned by her words. Why would she make marriage sound so... unreasonable? Although he had never imagined himself married, with a wife and children, he considered what that life might be like. He didn't find the image so very awful. Indeed, he rather liked the idea of sharing a bed with Lydia. Rather liked the idea of a babe bouncing on his bent foot whilst its tiny hands were curled around his forefingers, its shrieks of delight filling a room, its giggles ...

Adonis blinked. *Where the hell had that image come from?* He had never seen a member of the *ton* do such a thing. Never even heard a babe giggle.

Milton Grandby, Earl of Torrington, often spoke of doing such things with his cousin's children, though, his face lit up with such delight, his audience was left wondering why it was the earl had waited so long to marry. Even now, the man hadn't yet fathered an heir. Whenever he did, Adonis was quite sure the progeny would be spoiled rotten.

A hand waved in front of his face, bringing him back to the here and now.

"You're doing it again," Lydia complained as she stared at him.

Adonis blinked and returned the stare.

"Where *were* you?" she demanded, placing a steaming cup of tea in front of him.

"Imagining a babe bouncing on my boot," he replied quickly, not having the wherewithal to consider how his words might sound to the widowed viscountess.

Lydia blinked at the odd response. *Whatever had the man thinking of babies at a time like this?* "Oh," was all she could manage in response just then. "Well, before you go off fathering bastards, we have a puzzle to solve," she reminded him.

Adonis nodded, his attention going to the seemingly hundreds of pieces that lay scattered before him.

"Do you require something stronger than tea?" she asked again, settling herself into the chair opposite from the knight. "I have some scotch on the sideboard. Brandy, too."

"I do not," Adonis replied, his gaze darting over the collection of puzzle pieces. He helped himself to a hunk of cheese and took a sip of tea before he leaned closer to study the pieces.

Lydia dared a glance at him, wondering what he was thinking. *Whatever had the man imagining a babe bouncing on his boot?*

When the knight suddenly stood up, and then used his cane to climb atop the chair he had been sitting in to stare down at the tabletop, Lydia pushed away from the table and stepped back. *What the hell?*

"This isn't a map," Adonis announced. He stepped down

from the chair, his good leg and his cane providing support as he did so.

"Words? Or a drawing?" Lydia responded. She didn't admit she had done the same thing earlier that afternoon.

Adonis glanced at her. "Aye, possibly to both," he replied. He began rearranging the wood scraps, his deft fingers moving the pieces about the table until two or three formed the shapes of cursive letters. Lydia followed suit, a few more letters becoming apparent.

Over the course of the next hour, the two worked in relative silence as the scripted words spelled out the most unexpected phrase Lydia had ever read.

"Congratulations on your exceptional teamwork. A new assignment will be forthcoming. C." The entire phrase was surrounded by an oval line.

Adonis lifted his eyes to regard the viscountess. "What do you suppose he has in mind for us next?" he asked as he helped himself to a slice of ham.

Lydia shook her head as she pushed away from the table. "I've absolutely no idea, but I intend to let him know we have solved this particular puzzle." Adonis struggled to stand as she made her way to the escritoire. He watched as she pulled out a sheet of parchment in one hand and picked up an ink pot and pen with the other. "What, pray tell, should we tell the man?" she asked as she returned and resumed her seat.

Adonis settled back into his chair, not about to mention thanking the director for having coerced Lydia to seek his help on the puzzle. The man's note to her made it clear she had to include Adonis in the puzzling solving. "Admonish him, of course," he spoke as he leaned forward. "His instructions could have embroiled you in scandal—"

"As if your midnight visits do not?" she interrupted as she took pen to paper and began writing.

Adonis sighed. "I will not be caught entering or leaving your house, my lady," he murmured in assurance. "So let us hope his next assignment is something we can do without being seen."

A frisson shot through Lydia just then. Did the man realize what he suggested? Something clandestine? Something secret? Something done in dark corners or behind closed doors?

She had a brief moment of imagining the two of them in her bed, Adonis' lips grazing over her body, occasionally stopping to kiss a nipple or suckle a sensitive spot. Oliver had never been able to get that part quite right, the man so eager for his own release he barely spent any time in the foreplay she found to be the best part of lovemaking.

Jasper had been better at it. Better at the kissing and teasing, better at bringing her to a quick and sharp release before he plunged himself into her, but even he wasn't a skilled lover.

For some reason, Adonis struck her as a man who could be, and not just because he was a beautiful man. There was something about his eyes. Something about the way he gazed at objects, the way he studied them as his well-manicured fingers touched them. She could imagine him touching her with those fingers. Her nipples. Her womanhood. Her entire body. The shiver of delight she felt in response nearly had her gasping.

"Where *were* you just then?" Adonis asked in a whisper, his words spoken exactly as Lydia had said them when they were on the banks of the Serpentine.

Lydia blinked. And blinked again as she considered how to respond. "In my bed," she replied with an arched eyebrow. "About to go to sleep."

It wasn't a complete lie at least. She was sure Adonis could already read the tells that gave her away. Despite the long periods when he seemed to take leave of his senses, the man was still rather observant. He had to be if he had been an operative for the Foreign Office.

Adonis still held the slice of ham between his fingers, but he finally placed it on a piece of bread and took a bite, his eyes closing as he did. "Thank you for the late supper, my lady. I find myself rather hungry given I did not join my sister and Lord Craven for their dinner this evening. I find myself rather opposed to her censure," he whispered. "She thinks I belong in Bedlam."

Lydia ignored the comment about Bedlam—she was afraid she might agree with Lady Craven just to be polite. She poured him another cup of tea, the last of the pot dribbling into his cup. "It was the least I could do, given our assignment," she finally replied. She glanced at the clock over the fireplace. "It's nearly two. I suppose you should be taking your leave—"

"I will not leave this house until dawn, my lady," he interrupted.

"The locksmith was here this morning. Before you, I have never had a thief enter the household," she argued.

"And you still have not." He paused a moment, realizing her implication. "I am not a thief."

Angling her head to one side, Lydia sighed. "Tell me why."

"Please, my lady. Allow me to do what I promised," he begged.

Lydia furrowed her brows, wondering if the man intended to visit her house every night for the rest of her life. "Is it true? What you said about to whom you made the promise to provide protection?" she asked, hoping he would see to providing a straight answer.

Adonis dipped his head. "Your late husband, of course," he replied, his gaze not meeting hers.

Not completely surprised by his answer, Lydia still gave a start. "How did you even *know* him?" Just because her husband had at one time taken orders from Lord Chamberlain didn't mean that Sir Donald and Jasper knew each other from the Foreign Office.

Jasper had been a commander in the British Army, one of the few aristocrats to serve under Wellington in the later battles against Napoleon's forces on the Continent. How likely was it, then, for the two men to even know one another?

Unless Sir Donald also served under Wellington.

"We had... similar orders... in the Netherlands, my lady," Adonis replied in a hoarse whisper. "I will say nothing more on the matter."

Anger filled Lydia just then. "Similar orders?" she repeated, her voice no longer a whisper. "So, you... you *knew* him?"

Adonis sighed. "I did. Well, I knew of him, of course. And then I met him... on the way to Ligny."

Lydia hissed. Jasper had died sometime during the Battle of Ligny, although there was a caveat that he might have died the morning after. She could never get a straight answer from the War Office on the matter, and Lord Chamberlain certainly hadn't provided any intelligence on the matter. Until she had seen the drawing Chamberlain had showed her, she didn't even know for certain how Jasper had died.

"Was he a good commander?" she asked in a strangled whisper. *Jesus.* It had been a year. She could hardly believe she still felt sorrow over his loss.

Not expecting the question, Adonis furrowed his brows. "He was, as a matter of fact. He understood strategy. Understood war," he replied in hoarse whisper. "In the event you were not informed, he died of a bayonet wound." He didn't add that he thought the commander had also taken a musket ball in one of his shoulders.

Lydia stared at Adonis, wondering if he could read her mind. "I was not, at least, not until a few days ago," she replied, the catch in her voice a telltale sign she was about to cry. "Did he die alone?"

The knight considered how to respond. "No."

Nodding, Lydia finally pushed away from the table and picked up the tea tray from the table. "I am tired. I'm going up to bed. Do what you must," she managed around a sob that threatened to rob her of voice.

Adonis watched her go, rather surprised she didn't order

him to leave her house and threaten him with a visit from a constable. Or a Bow Street Runner.

Giving one last glance at the completed puzzle, he lifted its pasteboard box and placed it against the edge of the card table. With a few swipes of his hand, he had the pieces collected in the box and the lid placed over the top. Leaning back in his chair, he drained his tea and pondered what to do next.

He had a promise to keep. He was already in the house. After finishing off the last of the cheese, Adonis took the tray to the kitchen and then made his way to the mistress suite by going up the main stairs.

Adonis wasn't surprised to find Lydia already in her bed, her discarded gown draped over a shin toaster and her petticoats, corset, chemise and stockings dribbling over the edge of the bed.

The thought of her having undressed just the moment before his arrival had his cock hardening.

Christ!

It wasn't supposed to be like this. He wasn't supposed to find her attractive. Beautiful. Alluring.

Vulnerable.

Jasper's descriptions had suggested someone quite different. But why? Did the commander think Adonis would pursue Lady Barrymore for himself if he knew the truth?

Not possible. He was quite sure the viscount thought Adonis would die on the very same battlefield. The man had seen the shin bone jutting from the front of his broken leg, a horse having stepped on it during the heat of the battle.

Adonis had to jerk his head in an attempt to shake away the thought that had his leg throbbing in pain.

Lydia. Think of Lydia.

He had half a mind to join her in the bed, if for no other reason than to hold her. Comfort her. Kiss her hair and see her off to sleep as he had done the night before.

She was still grieving over the loss of her husband, if he understood her quiet sobs as she left the parlor. He could understand that feeling. Understand how bereft it made a person feel to have the only person in the world for whom one felt affection taken away in an act of violence.

Johanna had been that one for him.

As he settled into the upholstered Greek lounging chair by the window, Adonis allowed his mind to wander, to remember those days in the Netherlands, the weeks of innocence before he had to make his way to Brussels and report for duty to Wellington.

His favorite days.

Tears were streaming down his face when he finally fell asleep.

CHAPTER 22
IN THE STILL OF THE NIGHT

An hour later
Lydia held her breath for a moment, swallowing the last of a sob as she listened intently. She was sure Adonis was in the bedchamber, but if so, his entrance had been so quiet, she wasn't completely sure he was there.

Turning over so she faced him, she barely opened her eyes. His silhouette was evident in front of the window—the embers from the fireplace still lit the room in a golden-red glow—as was the barely audible sound of his labored breathing. Alarmed, she lifted herself onto one elbow and listened intently. She could swear she heard the man sniffling, heard the evidence of a sob or two.

Lydia stepped out of the bed and moved to stand before him, much like she had done the few nights before. Knowing she had nothing to fear from the man, she left the gun behind this time.

Although his eyes were closed, she could see the evidence of tears streaming down his cheeks. Lowering herself to the cushion next to his, Lydia reached out with a hand and used a thumb to brush away the moisture from one temple. When he didn't react nor move to indicate he was aware of her presence, she lifted her other hand and swept away the tears from the other cheek.

His hand gripped her wrist as his eyes flew open. "Johanna?" he said in a rather loud voice, his body straightening on the Greek lounging chair.

Lydia let out a slight shriek at his sudden movement, her body jerking in response. "Oh, my God, you scared me," she murmured, the words sounding breathless in the near-dark.

Adonis gulped and regarded her with wide eyes. When he glanced about the bedchamber, he finally dared a breath and relaxed a bit. "I... I apologize. I..." He allowed the sentence to trail off, his face betraying his disappointment at discovering he wasn't where he thought he was.

"Who is Johanna?" The words were spoken in a whisper, and Lydia struggled to keep a hiccup from sounding in her query. She didn't know why she felt the sudden pang of jealousy just then. Adonis meant nothing to her. Not in that way, at least.

His gaze having come to rest on Lydia's wrist—he still held it quite firmly—Adonis considered how to respond. "A woman I once knew," he finally whispered. "She's of no consequence now," he added as he let go of Lydia. "I fear I may have left a bruise."

Lydia used her other hand to rub the ring around her wrist where his fingers had gripped her. "I'll be fine." She paused a moment. "What do you mean she's of no consequence?"

Adonis pulled a handkerchief from his waistcoat pocket and wiped his nose. "She's... she's dead," he managed to get out without his voice breaking.

The image of Johanna had been so vivid in his mind's eye, he was sure she was real. Alive. Smiling at him as she did those few days when the two of them had made the best of what must have been a terrifying ordeal for her.

And then she was gone.

I loved her, Adonis thought then, blinking as he felt the tears return. He had never before cried over the loss of Johanna. Had he been ten minutes earlier in arriving at the hovel she had called home, he would have been dead, too.

But then he would have been spared from the Battle of Ligny. Spared from the agony of his leg wound and the months spent in a hospital in Brussels. Spared from having made the promise that had him spending his nights in the company of a woman who did not want his protection.

Probably didn't need it.

A hand waved in front of his face, and he frowned. "I was dreaming," he murmured.

"Having a nightmare is more like it," Lydia countered, disappointed when he didn't offer more information about Johanna. "Where *were* you?"

Weary, Adonis allowed a sigh. "The Kingdom of the Netherlands. Or whatever they're calling it these days," he replied with another sigh. "Somewhere north of Antwerp."

Lydia tried to imagine a map of the area. *North of Brussels. Not far from where Jasper had died.* "Did Lord Chamberlain assign you there?"

Adonis shook his head. "No. I had just arrived on a ship and was making my way to a rendezvous point near Brussels... I had some time, though. I couldn't get there too early or I might be caught by the enemy, and..." He sighed again.

"Who was she?"

Tears nearly threatened again, but Adonis swallowed hard and cleared his throat. "A young widow. Quite beautiful. From what I could gather, her husband's family had always been the caretakers of a windmill. When he died during one of the early battles with France, she was left there alone." He sniffled before using his handkerchief again. "She lived in the base of the windmill. Damnedest thing I've ever seen."

Lydia hissed, quite sure she could guess what might have happened to the poor woman. "Did you have to... save her... from the French?"

Adonis dipped his head. "I dispatched two with bullets and the third with a bayonet," he whispered after a time. "She couldn't manage on her own, of course—there was far too much to do to keep the damn windmill running—so I did what I could. The French forces were so scattered, but I truly thought they would head farther south. Go back to be closer to their own border. But while I was in Antwerp to locate some parts..." He paused, struggling to catch his breath. "And to meet my contact—I knew I needed to meet up with Wellington's man at some point—they shot a cannon ball into the windmill."

Oliver Preston had been there. The man had as much as admitted that he had helped the French that day.

Lydia gasped. "With her inside?" she guessed in a whisper. Her hand went to cover her mouth.

Adonis managed a nod. "I don't know if they knew she was in there, or if they determined it was where their men had been killed and they sought revenge, but when I found her, she was beneath so much rubble, I could not get her out," he said in a hoarse whisper. "The attack was my cue, of course. I had to get to Wellington while he was still in Brussels. So I left her. I left her there. God help me."

Lydia's arms were around his shoulders in an instant, pulling hard so her body pressed against his. "I'm so sorry, Adonis," she whispered, stunned when she felt one of his arms wrap around her back. Her head ended up against one of his shoulders, her face beneath his. "There was nothing you could have done..."

"I should have taken her away from there," he countered. "Settled her in the city before I met my contact."

Lydia didn't offer an alternative. The man would forever blame himself for something he couldn't have prevented.

She stiffened then, realizing why it was so necessary he keep his promise to provide protection for her. *Guilt*, she reasoned as she lifted her face to regard him. "When you stare into space like you do sometimes, are you thinking of her?" she asked in a quiet voice.

Adonis sighed. "Sometimes," he finally replied. "She... she seemed happy during the fortnight I was with her. Despite her lot in life, she always had a smile for me."

The pang of jealousy surprised Lydia again. "Were you two... lovers?"

"Morning and night," Adonis replied with a quick nod, a smile finally appearing to lift his entire face.

Lydia was quite sure she had never seen a more beautiful man at that moment. Beautiful and broken, and yet holding her as if his very life depended on it. Perhaps it did. "I am truly sorry for your loss," she murmured.

She felt his nod and how his arm seemed to tighten around her shoulders. Sure he kissed her hair, or perhaps merely settled his head atop hers, Lydia was reminded she hadn't braided it. This would be one night it would remain loose.

"Come to bed. We're both exhausted," she whispered as she moved to get up. When Adonis didn't lessen his hold on her, she gave him a questioning glance. "What is it?"

"May I hold you? Whilst you sleep?" he whispered.

A frisson shot through Lydia just then, the thought of his body pressed against hers a rather pleasant one. Even now, there was something positively scandalous and yet so comforting at having him hold her as he was doing. "Of course," she replied. "Just be sure to take off your boots before you get into bed."

Adonis allowed her to remove herself from his hold and return to the bed. He watched as she settled into the mattress, her body well past the middle of the bed when she pulled the bed linens and counterpane over her shoulder. She gave a glance back in his direction. "Are you coming?"

The knight removed his boots and gave a thought to removing far more, but in the end, tiredness had him simply crawling into the bed fully clothed. With a sigh, he draped an arm over Lydia's middle and pulled her against the front of his body. He was asleep before he realized he held one of her breasts in his hand.

CHAPTER 23
A KERFUFFLE IN THE COACH

The following night, June 22, 1816

Lydia took one last look in the cheval mirror as she threaded wires through the piercings in her ears. A set of crystal chandeliers then dangled from her plump earlobes, their multifaceted surfaces reflecting the candlelight. The matching necklace graced her neck, a gift from Jasper on the occasion of their first wedding anniversary.

The gown she wore was appropriate for the theatre, but showed her décolletage only when she leaned forward, a pose she expected to employ frequently that night. If Adonis Truscott even once attempted to get lost in his thoughts, Lydia had every intention of bringing him back to the here and now with a few well placed fingers and a reason to stay in the present.

After last night's session of puzzle solving, Lydia found herself rather torn about the man and his mission. As she feared, the man seemed intent on providing protection for her, perhaps for the rest of her life.

If he did so whilst in her bed, she doubted she would have any reason to complain. After he had joined her, after he had pulled her body against his and wrapped his arm around her and held her in a cocoon of comfort, she had slept so soundly, she was completely unaware of when he had taken his leave of her. It had probably been at dawn, she reasoned, but she remembered waking and wishing he were still there.

"Oh, who am I trying to bamboozle?" she asked herself in a whisper just as Rachel reappeared in her bedchamber with a length of silk that matched her gown.

"I found it, milady," the maid announced happily.

Lydia straightened and regarded the sapphire watered silk with an appreciative eye. "I don't remember ever having worn it," she murmured.

Rachel gave a shrug. "I don't either, milady."

Wrapping the shawl about her shoulders, Lydia decided it would hide the top of her gown until it was advantageous to remove it. Probably after the play had begun. Certainly after Sir Donald had joined her in the box.

Whatever was she thinking to attempt seduction with the knight? After what had happened the night before, seduction seemed unnecessary. What new information did she hope to learn with such a bold move?

Lydia sighed and made her way down the stairs and to the vestibule. Although Jenkins held a mantle, she shook her head. "Not tonight," she said as she sailed out the front door and hurried to the waiting town coach. Although she couldn't see her breaths in the night air, it was rather chilly. She almost turned back for the mantle, but remembered why it would be counter to what she hoped to achieve.

Stepping into the dark town coach, Lydia frowned when she realized the exterior lanterns weren't lit. She was about to chide the driver when she realized she wasn't alone.

"I nearly sat on you," she murmured as she settled into the squabs.

"I was rather hoping you would."

The sound of Oliver Preston's voice should have sent shivers down her spine. Should have had her breathless with anticipation of whatever he had planned for the two of them as the coach made its way to Drury Lane. But Lydia found herself feeling annoyed.

Even more annoyed than she used to feel when thinking of Adonis Truscott.

"I thought you would be on your wedding trip by now," Lydia whispered. "Whatever are you *doing* in here?"

Oliver managed a look of hurt that Lydia could make out despite the darkened interior of the coach. "Hoping to steal a kiss or two... or more," he said in that voice he used when he thought he was being irresistible. "I leave in the morning."

Rather disgusted by the rogue's behavior, Lydia rolled her eyes. "You are a married man now, Oliver. Except for an occasional dance at a ball, I intend to have nothing to do with you."

"Oh, Lydia, my darling..." Oliver started to argue. But Lydia would have none of it. She was supposed to be on a mission tonight. The last thing she needed was the distraction of a man who was supposed to be a newlywed—and out of her life.

"Now get out of this coach before I have my driver bodily remove you," she warned in a voice loud enough to be overheard by the driver.

"Really, Lydia. You're being unreasonable," Oliver argued.

The door to the town coach suddenly opened.

"The lady has made her wishes known, sir. You would be wise to honor them."

Lydia blinked when she realized the voice wasn't that of her driver but rather belonged to someone else.

Oliver dared a glance toward the open door but didn't see who stood beyond the opening. "Perhaps when I return from my trip to the Continent—"

"Perhaps not, Oliver. Really, sir, you're a married man now, and I'm not about to allow you to make an adulteress out of me," Lydia managed with a good deal of venom.

Giving her a look of offense, Oliver stepped out of the coach and closed the door with a slam just as the opposite door opened and Adonis Truscott stepped in and closed the door behind him. He used his cane to tap the ceiling and the coach lurched forward just as he took a seat across from a rather stunned Lydia.

"I do hope the rake didn't manage anything untoward, my lady," he said in a low voice.

Lydia blinked. "I wouldn't have allowed it," she replied with a shake of her head. "How...?" She paused, realizing just then that Adonis had obviously been waiting to follow her to the theatre—or perhaps he had intended to ride with her all along. "Where is your horse?"

"In the mews behind my apartments, of course," he replied, his eyes widening. "At least, I expect that's where he is."

She gave a huff. "And if Mr. Preston hadn't left this coach? What then? Would you have *walked* to the theatre?"

This seemed to have the knight a bit shocked. "Of course not. I would have seen to his removal with a right cross to his jaw. Then, if your ladyship didn't care for my company either, I would have hired a hackney," he claimed with a sigh. "Thank you, my lady, for saving me from having to do so, as I find them rather... unpleasant."

Lydia rolled her eyes, knowing the reaction would go unseen in the dark coach. She couldn't blame him for his opinion of hackneys. She found them rather unpleasant as well, and silently thanked Jasper for having left her a comfortable town coach.

As for what the knight might have done to Oliver had he not taken his leave of the coach, she rather wished she could have paid witness to Sir Donald's right cross and the stunned expression Oliver would have sported directly afterwards. "You're welcome, Sir Donald." She regarded him in the dim light, rather surprised how handsome he appeared. Not beautiful, with the planes of his face darkened as they were, but rather dangerous.

The knight made a sound of surprise. Lydia couldn't quite make out what he was doing until his cape coat was draped over her shoulders. "Your butler should have offered you a mantle, my lady," he murmured, the censure clear in his voice.

Lydia angled her head as she breathed in the scent of his familiar cologne. "He did," she replied simply.

The knight settled back into the seat opposite of her and regarded her with a quizzical brow. "You don't find the evening rather chilly?" he asked.

Allowing a small smile, Lydia gave a shrug. "I do, actually. But by wearing a mantle, I take away the opportunity for a gentleman to practice chivalry." She heard the catch in Adonis' breath and silently congratulated herself on having surprised the knight. "Thank you for reinforcing my good opinion of your sex."

"Do you include Mr. Preston in your estimation?"

Lydia shook her head. "I do not, but then I do not think him a gentleman, either."

"And yet you would share your bed with him." The statement didn't hold a hint of question, but was said more as an accusation.

A flash of anger had Lydia about to slap the knight across the face. *How did he know?* She had told no one of the brief *affaire*—not even her best friends. She was fairly sure her servants were unaware of Oliver when he'd been in her bedchamber. So how had Adonis discovered the *affaire?* "I admit to having done so on a few occasions," she countered, her voice taking on an icy edge. "But if you were eavesdropping on the conversation we were having a few minutes ago, you would know the man is no longer welcome—in my conveyance or in my bed," she stated firmly.

Adonis allowed a sigh. "Thank the gods. I was quite sure I was going to find myself in Wimbledon Common on the morrow."

Lydia blinked. And blinked again. "Are you saying you would have challenged the man to a duel?" she asked in a startled whisper. In the light of a gas lamp the coach passed just then, she saw Adonis give a nod as one of his eyebrows arched up.

"Aye. And since I am a crack shot, I expect Mr. Preston would be quite dead at one minute past dawn."

A shiver shot up Lydia's spine just then.

Fright?

No.

Excitement?

Somewhat.

Satisfaction, actually. "I would have liked to be a witness to such a scene, Sir Donald. As you have probably already surmised, I find I do not like Mr. Preston's company."

The knight did not respond, and for a moment, Lydia thought he was lost in his thoughts. But Adonis leaned forward and placed a gloved hand on her knee. Lydia nearly gave a start at the sudden touch. "Have you threatened him with your flintlock?" he asked in a hoarse whisper.

Lydia had half a mind to tell the knight she'd *shot* Oliver just to see how he would react, but she opted to act coy. "Perhaps," she answered with an arched brow.

"I would have liked to be a witness to such a scene, milady," he whispered. "But I suppose I must allow my imagination to complete the image. A rather easy task given I've already been the subject of your steady aim."

Sighing, Lydia was about to apologize for having threatened him when she remembered just how incensed she had been at finding him in her bedchamber. Now, she realized she would miss him if he wasn't in it every night.

The town coach halted, and a quick glance out the window had Lydia realizing they were already at the theatre. "How shall we do this?" she asked.

Adonis gave a shrug. "I was hoping to escort you to your box. That is, if you don't mind terribly... being seen in my company," he replied in his most unsure manner.

A slow smile appeared on Lydia's face. There would be gossip, she realized, but perhaps not as much as she originally thought. She was no longer in mourning. "I do not mind a bit."

Giving her a nod, Adonis stepped down from the coach and turned to assist her.

He did so at exactly the same time as several other gentlemen did, up and down the row of equipage lining the street. Given the sudden crowd entering the theatre all at the same time, the pair's entry into the lobby went unnoticed.

CHAPTER 24
A NIGHT AT THE THEATRE

A few minutes later

Despite the chilly evening, a larger than normal crowd assembled for the performance of "Bertram, or the Castle of St. Aldobrand" at the Theatre Royal in Drury Lane. Once Adonis had them through one of the sets of double-doors at the top of the stairs, Lydia paused and indicated Adonis should take back his coat. He did so, but not before leaning over to whisper, "Your gown is stunning, milady."

A shiver at hearing the way he said the words had Lydia wondering if she should have kept the coat. "Thank you, Sir Donald." She noted his evening clothes, the black satin breeches and tailcoat perfectly tailored, his silver waistcoat embroidered in silver and white silk. The only out-of-place piece of clothing was a bright red woolen scarf. "Your tailor is to be commended. Weston, perhaps?"

Adonis blinked. "Garth, actually, although I've had yet to pay a call on his shop since my return," he remarked.

Lydia considered the comment. What had the man been doing for the two months since his return to England?

Being lost in his thoughts, she remembered.

"My box is this way," she indicated as she placed a hand on his proffered arm. They made their way toward the stairs leading to the upper stories, their path slowed by clusters of patrons engaged in conversations. Although she paid witness to Lord and Lady Torrington in the company of Lord and Lady Norwick, she didn't stop to greet them, and then pretended not to notice a few ladies she had seen at the garden party.

"Are you... embarrassed at being seen in my company?" Adonis asked as they made their way.

Lydia stiffened and nearly paused mid-step. "Certainly not. Why would you think such a thing?"

The knight glanced in her direction before replying. "Because everyone who has been in my sister's company for the past two months has been told I am mad, and I am quite sure it would be in your best interest not to be seen in my company."

"And yet you rode in my town coach and escorted me into the theatre," Lydia countered, one eyebrow arched up.

Adonis blinked. "True. There are times I forget..." He stepped around a couple who had stopped so the lady could retrieve one of her slippers. "That I forget I am supposed to act a certain way. In order to meet *expectations*," he clarified quickly, giving an arched brow to match the one Lydia had aimed in his direction. They headed down the narrow hall behind the second-story boxes.

"To which expectations are you referring?" Lydia asked as they reached the door to her box. Adonis opened it and stepped aside as she entered into a space that could easily seat six or more people. Although she could have moved all the way to front—there would be no one else sharing her box this evening—she elected to take a seat in the second row. The stage was still visible from the vantage, but her action seemed to reinforce what Adonis had implied earlier.

Taking the seat next to hers, Adonis angled his head. "Those that would have me a candidate for Bedlam," he answered in a quiet voice.

Her gaze having swept what she could see of the theatre's audience, Lydia jerked her attention to his face. "You're saying you've been... *playing* at being insane?" she countered in a hoarse whisper. The idea was so ludicrous, she nearly accused him of being mad right then and there.

"For my sister's sake, yes," he acknowledged. "She caught me staring at nothing at all—"

"As have I," Lydia interrupted.

"And I didn't immediately respond to her question because I... I preferred being where I was. *When* I was," he corrected himself. He turned in his chair to better face Lydia. "Milady, I know this sounds... mad, but because she caught me doing it three or four times, she was convinced I was insane, and she began telling everyone who would listen that I was mad. If I were to act... *normal*, then those people would think my sister the mad one," he explained with a wave of his hand.

Lydia blinked. And blinked again. "That's the most ridiculous reasoning I've ever heard," she replied.

"I know," Adonis acknowledged with a nod. "But what was I to do?"

A bell sounded and the noise level in the theatre quieted as Lydia considered how to respond. "Does she know you're not insane? Now, I mean?" she whispered, leaning in his direction so her lips nearly touched his ear.

Well aware of how close she was, Adonis couldn't help but notice how she had allowed her shawl to drop from her shoulders, how her décolletage was on display for his eyes only. How her collarbones were highlighted in the dim lighting.

What was the question?

An actor appeared on the stage, and applause sounded from below.

"You're doing it again," Lydia accused, turning to stare at him.

"I assure you, I am not," he countered. "It's just..." He closed his eyes, as if he had to break the spell she had over him. "You're just so damned bewitching," he whispered. "I want nothing more than to be in your company. All the time. He warned me, you know," he added as he turned to face the stage. "He tried to make you out to be some sort of siren. But he was not nearly as stern with his warning as he should have been."

Lydia stared at Adonis for several seconds, realizing he spoke of her late husband. *Bewitching?* Jasper had never accused her of such a thing.

"I am not a witch," she whispered, rather stunned by his words. By their implication.

Adonis turned to face her, his lips mere inches from hers. "Then how do you explain your effect on me, my lady?"

Lydia found she needed the warmth of the shawl, and brought it up to cover her shoulders. Unable to form a suitable response—how could she answer such a question?—she turned to face the stage, allowing the actors' words to pull her into the story.

Realizing he had spoiled the mood with his words, Adonis turned his body to face the stage. Instead of paying attention to the play, though, he allowed himself the time to form an apology and was, after a time and despite his best efforts, lost in thought.

CHAPTER 25
ANOTHER INTRUDER

*L*ater that night
Dismissing her maid almost as soon as she returned from the theatre—Lydia was quite sure she would have help with her gown as soon as Adonis could make it into the house without alerting anyone to his presence—Lydia moved to her dressing table. She regarded her image in the looking glass as she pulled off the diamond earbobs and necklace she had worn that night.

Jasper had given them to her on the occasion of their first anniversary. *For putting up with me,* he had said whilst they dined at the Carleton Hotel. It was the first time she felt like a viscountess, that moment he had draped the necklace around the long column of her neck and attached each of the earbobs in place of the set made of paste. He had ordered champagne that night, claiming he should see to it they had champagne every night. But there was rarely a bottle in the cellar, and Lydia couldn't remember another occasion at which he drank a glass.

Lydia glanced down at her gown, realizing she had worn the same gown that night as well. The bright sapphire blue watered silk shimmered on its own without any jewels, but the diamonds had provided a glittering finish.

Perhaps that's what had the men in her life bewitched, she reasoned. Not her so much as what she wore.

No. That couldn't be it. Adonis had been most apologetic with her during that evening's intermission. *When I accused you of bewitching me, I did not mean it in a manner meant as an accusation so much as an admission that I have developed feelings for you*, he had said. *Please forgive me.* He had said the words before most of the patrons in the theatre stood up to stretch their legs and to visit with others behind their boxes.

They, too, had stood up, but not to leave the box. Instead, he had taken her into his arms and kissed her in the darkest corner of the box. She had allowed it because if he hadn't been the one to initiate the kiss, she would have. When the bell sounded and it was time to return to their seats, they had instead taken their leave of the theatre, saying not a word to one another.

Lydia allowed the shawl to fall from her arms, draping it over the back of her dressing table chair. About to pull the gown from her body, she was aware of a *thump* in a nearby room. She stilled her movements, wondering if she was merely hearing her maid—Rachel's room was on the third story—but when she didn't hear anything more, she relaxed. Hurrying to her bedchamber door, she checked the handle to be sure the door was unlocked. Adonis would no doubt see to locking it after he arrived.

When another *thump* and a slight squeaking noise came from farther down the hall from her bedchamber, Lydia stilled her movements. She recognized the squeaking noise. Jasper's bedchamber door made that noise. Barely felt footfalls vibrated through the carpet beneath her feet.

Adonis wouldn't come through that bedchamber. Jenkins would be abed by now, as would Rachel. No one from the staff should have been up and about, and certainly not in Jasper's bedchamber.

Lydia released the breath she'd been holding and took another. Oliver had been in her coach that evening. He had obviously climbed into it after her driver parked it in front of the townhouse.

Or had he been in there from the time it left the mews behind the house?

When the squeaking door clicked into place, Lydia squared her shoulders. *Damn him!*

Moving back to her dressing table, Lydia picked up the candle lamp before palming her gun from beneath the pillow. She slid it into a pocket as she made her way to her dressing room door.

"Oliver? Is that you?" Lydia called out in a hoarse whisper meant to sound light and hopeful. She stopped just inside the dressing room door on the end closest to the master suite, the flame from the lamp she carried barely providing a pool of light around her. The glint of metal in the intruder's hand suggested he held a weapon.

"Christ, Lydia. You scared me nearly to death!"

Oh, if only I had, Lydia nearly replied. Instead, she moved farther into the bedchamber. "Whatever are you doing here, Oliver?" she asked, making sure her voice could be overheard by Adonis if he had managed to make it to her bedchamber. She was sure he was in the house by now.

Oliver Preston sighed, half tempted to claim he was trying to make his way to her bedchamber by way of Jasper's. "I don't suppose you'd believe I was on my way to ravish you," he said in a voice tinged with forced humor.

Lydia felt annoyance far beyond any she had felt when in the company of Adonis, but she held her tongue and forced herself to sound reasonable. "I know I made myself quite clear about our arrangement when you agreed to marry another," she replied curtly. "As well as in the coach earlier tonight. So, since you cannot be here to ravish me, why *are* you here?"

Oliver let out an audible sigh. "Truth be told, I'm still in search of that item I spoke with you about a few days ago. That item that belonged to your late husband."

The alarm bells not already sounding in her head started

to ring. Loudly. "Well, I do hope your wife doesn't know you've come. It would be horrid if she thought we were still having our... *affaire*," Lydia said in a quiet voice she hoped Adonis wouldn't overhear. *Please be here!*

The intruder let out a huff as he moved to a tall chest of drawers. "Come now, Lydia. Effie knows nothing, nor will she," he replied in a low voice. He opened a drawer and pushed a few things around, cursing under his breath.

"Perhaps if I knew exactly what you were looking for, I could help find it," Lydia suggested, moving to her husband's wardrobe. The pool of light illuminated the small pistol Oliver had placed atop the chest of drawers. *Why the hell did he think he needed a gun?*

"Barrymore was supposed to leave me a *ring*," Oliver began in explanation. "It was... for a mission. I didn't think I would ever need it, what with everything that happened last year, but..." He paused a moment, as if he were trying to determine if he could tell her what he sought. "Now I find I do. I have a mission to complete before I can leave for the Continent."

Lydia angled her head, rather surprised the man would divulge his reason for being there so easily. "Is that why you were in the coach this evening?"

Oliver gave a shrug, opening another drawer. "I preferred to have your permission, of course," he replied. "Did he ever tell you about it? About the ring?"

Angling her head to one side, Lydia knew exactly which ring Oliver sought. Why Jasper would want him to have it, though, was beyond her reasoning just then. Her husband rather liked the ring, even if he didn't wear it very often. "Is it like a signet ring?" Lydia asked as she changed her direction and headed to her Jasper's jewelry box.

"Something like that," Oliver replied, turning his attention to another drawer.

"Does it have a gemstone on top?"

Oliver sighed. "I just know it's supposed to have a hinged

compartment. Really, Lydia, I can do this myself," he said with some impatience.

"Like this?" Lydia replied, ignoring his growing impatience. She pulled Jasper's favorite ring from his jewel box, her thumbnail popping open the hinged top that held what appeared to be a diamond but was really only paste. The compartment beneath, a tiny space that could hold several small gemstones or a tiny folded paper, was now apparently empty but for one tiny gemstone. She quickly closed it, palming most of what had been inside. "He used to hide sapphires in it when he was on smuggling missions," she murmured as she held it out to Oliver. "Used them as currency."

The man's eyes widened as he moved to take it from her. He frowned as he studied the ring. "How does it work?"

Lydia pointed to the sparkling paste. "It's set on a hinged box. Just give it a tug with your fingernail, and it should pop open. Be careful, though…"

Too late.

Oliver had managed to open the lid, but he wasn't expecting anything to fall out of it. "What was that?" he asked, his eyes darting about the Aubusson carpet near his boots.

Lydia sighed loudly. "Oh, probably just a diamond or perhaps a sapphire," Lydia said as she reached for the lamp. She slowly lowered it towards the floor, waving it about in attempt to illuminate whatever had fallen out. Once Oliver was down on one knee in his search for the gemstone, she used her own knee to kick him hard, just under his chin, so his head was forced up and backwards. The sound of teeth breaking preceded the man's tumble to the floor.

"Well, that was a bit more effective than what I planned to do to the bounder," Adonis said from where he stood in the doorway to the dressing room. He moved to where Oliver's gun rested on the chest of drawers and stuffed it into a pocket.

Lydia gave him a quelling glance before opening her

hand over the top of the chest of drawers to allow several gemstones to spill onto it. Then she pulled the drapery tieback from its hook next to the bedchamber's only window. "Here," she said as she held it out. "You can tie up his hands with this."

Adonis arched an eyebrow as he took the tasseled tieback from her. "Makes me wonder if you ever did this to Commander Barrymore," he murmured as he set about securing Oliver's hands behind his back. Lydia used the other tieback around the base of the intruder's boots, rather glad to see his boots were of a type that would require the help of a valet to remove.

"I was rarely in this room," she replied, wishing she had spent more time in it. More time in Jasper's bed. More time with Jasper. Perhaps if she had, she would have found herself with child. Would have born him an heir to carry on the Barrymore viscountcy. Would have a child to love and cherish.

How odd to think of babies at a time like this!

Aware his words weren't taken in the lighthearted manner they were meant, Adonis stilled his movements and regarded her for a moment. "I apologize. My remark was... rude," he whispered.

Lydia regarded him for a moment, rather surprised at his apology. "You're forgiven, of course. I rather doubt my late husband ever considered tying me to the bed. I have reason to believe he didn't think it appropriate to bed a wife the way he would his mistress."

Adonis' head jerked up. He stared at Lydia for a moment. "But the commander didn't have a mistress," he murmured.

Lydia blinked, rather stunned to hear the claim, and then even more stunned Adonis would know anything quite that personal about Jasper. "You seem very sure."

Adonis stilled himself, his body resting on the heels of his boots as he regarded her. "I am." His eyes seemed to glaze over, but before they could, Lydia reached out and grabbed his arm.

"Don't you dare," she hissed. "Don't you dare go to wher-ever it is you go when you're lost in thought," she warned, rising to her feet as the sudden anger threatened to have her yelling at him.

The knight stood up slowly, his head shaking slightly. "I am *here*, my lady," he said in a quiet voice. "I'm not going anywhere," he added as he moved to take her into his arms.

He kissed her then, a soft kiss that took her by surprise in how long he held it, in how gentle his pillowed lips pressed against hers, in how he barely pulled away to finally rest his forehead against hers. Their kisses at the theatre had been nothing like it. There, they had been forceful, possessive, as if he intended to brand her lips so that no one else could claim them.

"You had better not leave me given there's a rather fright-ening intruder in here," she murmured, her body finally relaxing against the front of his.

Adonis dared a glance at the unconscious man. "I think it's best we send for a Bow Street Runner," he commented. "He should be transported for what he's done, but I rather think Chamberlain will want him in Newgate."

Lydia's eyes widened. "But, didn't he work for Chamber-lain?" she whispered.

"Hardly. More like the French. At least, that's what Chamberlain always thought."

One hand going to her mouth, Lydia stared at Adonis even as she remembered Chamberlain's warning about the ring. "Oh, my God," she whispered. "He... he was a friend of Jasper, or so he claimed—"

"He was. To many," Adonis affirmed.

Lydia moved the hand to her middle, as if she might be sick. "I allowed him to... he... I shared my bed—"

"As you were supposed to," Adonis whispered, struggling to keep his sudden jealousy in check. The gun was in his pocket. He could easily shoot the man and claim he did so to protect Lydia.

Gasping, Lydia stepped away from the knight. "What are you saying?"

Realizing she was unaware of the roll she had played in trapping Oliver Preston, Adonis gave a shrug. "Chamberlain knew Preston was a spy for someone besides the Crown," he murmured. "We all had parts to play to see to it he was caught in the act. Even Jasper knew his friend was really his enemy."

Angry tears pricked the corners of Lydia's eyes. "Jasper knew? Why... why wasn't *I* told?"

Adonis moved to take her into his arms again, but Lydia backed away. "Don't touch me," she said through a clenched jaw.

Lowering his head, Adonis gave her a moment before saying, "Would you have been able to have an *affaire* with the man if you knew?"

"Of course not!" she replied, her hands clenched into fists, one of which brushed against the evidence of her gun in her pocket. She had half a mind to use it to shoot Oliver, her anger was so palpable. She closed her eyes then, realizing to what she had just admitted. Even if she had known it was her job to bed Oliver, she wouldn't have been able to carry out the assignment. "Dammit," she whispered as her arms wrapped around her middle.

"Your secret is safe with me," Adonis whispered as he finally drew her back into his arms.

Although she wanted nothing more than to be held, to have a good cry and get it over with, Lydia stiffened. "I want him out of here. Out of my life," she whispered hoarsely. When she stilled herself to listen intently, Adonis did the same.

Adonis gave up his hold on her and stepped back. "Someone's coming," he whispered.

Lydia nodded and moved to the door. "Jenkins, I think," she said in a hoarse whisper. "His quarters are directly above."

Moving into the dressing room, Adonis hid while Lydia opened the door and stepped aside.

"I've discovered the thief who broke the lock on the back door," she said in preamble, hoping Jenkins wouldn't be too stunned to find her in Jasper's bedchamber.

"Are you all right, my lady?" the butler asked as he waved his candle lamp in front of his body.

"Startled is all. I'm quite sure I'll need some brandy later, but for now, I need a footman to fetch a watchman or a constable and another to go to Bow Street."

Jenkins peered down at the trussed up man on the floor and then straightened. "Why, that's Mr. Preston, my lady."

"Yes, it is," Lydia admitted. "It seems he was after one of Jasper's rings," she said as her candle lamp illuminated the ring on the carpet. "I kicked him in the chin," she added, knowing Jenkins would wonder as to how the man ended up on the floor. She waved the lamp in a wider arc, determined to find whatever had remained in the ring when she dumped most of its contents into her hand.

The single sapphire she had left inside the ring's compartment lay next to a tiny piece of paper. She plucked the paper from where it rested and stuffed it into her pocket.

"I'll send both footmen right away, my lady," Jenkins said as he hurried to the door.

"I'll need a note delivered to Fitzsimmons House," she called out, "But it will take me some time to write it." Within minutes, the front door opened and shut, and Lydia watched the footmen make their way down the gas-lit street from where she stood in front of the bedchamber's only window.

Rachel, her eyes wide with fright, appeared in the open door. "Is your ladyship well?" she asked carefully.

Lydia turned, one arm held across her middle as the other gripped the drapery. "I am fine, really," she replied. She wasn't, but she wasn't about to turn into a watering pot just then. "You go on back to bed. Given how late it is, and how long it will take for the authorities to remove this miscreant, I expect I won't be up much before noon," she added as a hint that the maid need not attend her in the morning.

"Very good, my lady," Rachel said as she bobbed a curtsy and disappeared.

Adonis stepped from inside the dressing room. "We have a few moments before the constable comes," he said in a whisper. He pulled her into his arms and held her, as if he knew she would break down at any moment.

"Not yet. I have to write a note to Lord Chamberlain."

"That can wait until the morning," he replied. "Preston can spend the night in gaol." *And the rest of his life in hell*, he nearly added.

Giving into his hold on her, Lydia allowed him to support her until the arrival of the constable. At that point, Adonis moved into her bedchamber and settled onto the Greek lounging chair, rather annoyed he couldn't be of help with answering the questions the man put forth.

The Bow Street Runner wasn't far behind. Adonis had to smile when he heard Lydia drop Lord Chamberlain's name. She was no doubt angry with the viscount and had decided she had no qualms about the man being roused from his bed in the middle of the night.

He rather hoped Chamberlain was sharing his bed with his wife and had already managed a tumble or two. If not, the man would be in a bad mood for days.

Deciding there was nothing he could do until Lydia joined him, Adonis closed his eyes. He tried hard not to think of Johanna, but the night's events had brought her to the forefront of his memories once again.

*I*t was another hour before Preston was bodily removed from Jasper's bedchamber. A pair of constables did the work while the Runner gave orders. Having arrived within a few minutes of the first constable's appearance, he quickly took charge of the investigation. Lydia calmly answered his questions, although it became apparent early on that Lord Chamberlain's name would have to be spoken—the man seemed to think it was a simple robbery attempt rather than proof of a treasonous activity.

Preston was tossed into the back of a paddy wagon. At some point, the rogue had regained consciousness and claimed to be an agent of the Crown on assignment, but a swift kick to the jaw had silenced him—probably for the rest of the night given the stiff heel of Lydia's shoe. She had no desire to learn the man's fate, so she turned down the opportunity to ride with the Runner to pay witness to Preston's incarceration.

A few minutes after the household fell silent, Lydia finally returned to her own bedchamber.

CHAPTER 26
COMING TO TERMS WITH A STUBBORN MAN

"*A*re you there?"

Lydia's whispered query could barely be heard over the crackle of the small fire that warmed her bedchamber.

"I am, milady," Adonis replied as he straightened on the Greek lounging chair. "Is it all over?" he asked, his voice tinged with worry. He quickly wiped his face with the back of his hand, relieved to discover his tears had dried. "Is something wrong?"

There was a pause before Lydia moved to the edge of the chair, surprised by the sense of relief she felt at seeing him right where she expected him to be. "Not wrong, exactly. But I think it's past time..." She paused a moment and cursed herself for not being more forceful—more insistent—with the man. "We need to have a talk about your need to play midnight watchman on my behalf," she struggled to get out.

Adonis rested his elbows on his knees as he leaned forward. "My presence is not negotiable—"

"I know," Lydia interrupted him.

"I have made a promise that I intend—"

"I know all that. Now it's time we consider the full ramifications of your chivalry," Lydia stated.

"Ramifications?" Adonis repeated in a hoarse whisper.

"Yes." She paused when she noticed a satchel near his feet. "What's that?"

"A change of clothes. I shouldn't want to leave your house in formal attire," he replied, not bothering to add that his sketchpad was in there, as well. At some point, he thought he might spend part of his watch doing a drawing of Lydia. Although his attempts to draw had been almost primitive since Ligny, he thought his skills were improving. "It was in the coach."

"Oh." Well, the man certainly planned well. "Could you please... help me remove my gown and corset and join me in bed? We could talk out here, but it's much warmer under the quilts," she whispered.

Adonis blinked. Had he heard her correctly? She *wanted* him to join her in the bed? He was up and out of the Greek lounging chair in a move that belied his bad leg. He had the fastenings on the back of her gown undone in a moment, the layers of watered silk removed from her body in an instant after that.

The thump of her pistol against her thigh reminded her she had hidden it there. She turned and placed both hands on Adonis' shoulders to still his movements. "A moment, please."

"What was that?" he asked in a hoarse whisper, well aware of the dense weight somewhere in the watered silk.

"My gun." She took the gown from him and carefully removed the pistol, her fingers searching for the piece of paper she had plucked from the carpet earlier that night. "And a clue, I think," she added as she held up the folded paper."

Adonis stared at the tiny paper. "Where did you get that?"

Lydia moved closer to the fireplace, her corset-and-stocking clad body lit in a beautiful golden red as she unfolded the paper and held it to the light. "It was in Jasper's ring. Along with the sapphires," she murmured. She struggled to make out the tiny print on the paper, frustrated when she could not.

"May I?" Adonis whispered, his gaze coming from over her shoulder.

Lydia inhaled sharply, the scent of his cologne filling her nostrils. "Please."

Not moving from where he stood, Adonis peered at the paper, able to make out the word "traitor" on one side. On the other, he found "OP is a".

Gasping, Lydia pressed her back against Adonis, glad for the solidity of his body just then. "Jasper knew Oliver was a traitor. More than a year ago," she whispered.

Adonis wrapped an arm around her middle, not too terribly surprised by the news the ring had held. "I think Chamberlain suspected as much back then. He must have known Barrymore would leave word in the ring. It was his way of passing information."

"But why now?" Lydia asked. "It's been a year—"

"More. Commander Barrymore was on the Continent for nearly a month before he went into battle," Adonis reminded her. "Since he didn't take the ring, he made sure someone would find it. Oliver must have known what was in it—"

"Someone had to have told him—"

"Probably Commander Barrymore. Not directly, of course, but in a way that took months for the news to reach the bastard. He set a trap, actually." He paused a moment, his lips moving to kiss her temple. "He put you in a great deal of danger by leaving the ring here, though." *No wonder he wanted someone to provide protection for Lydia.*

Lydia allowed a sigh. "He knew I could take care of myself. He was the one who taught me how to shoot. How to kick a man."

Adonis decided not to remind her just then that Jasper Barrymore had demanded Adonis provide protection for his soon-to-be widow. The man had to have known Oliver

Preston would search for the ring—and do whatever he must to take possession of it.

Undoing the laces of her corset, Adonis said, "You have a rather effective kick, it's true."

"You'd be wise to remember that," Lydia murmured, although her voice was tinged with a hint of humor.

"I will, my lady."

Giving one last glance at the paper, she nearly tossed it into the flames, but Adonis caught her wrist before she could do so. "It's evidence against Preston," he reminded her.

Lydia nodded and instead set the paper on the nightstand. "You're right, of course. Chamberlain will want it." She pushed the corset from her body and tossed it onto the shin toaster. Although she should have been chilled to the bone—she wore only a chemise and stockings—she felt rather warm just then.

He lifted her body into his arms and moved to the side of the bed, placing her onto the expanse of white linen. He doffed his boots as he leaned the back of his thighs against the bed. Daring a backwards glance, he noticed how Lydia had moved to the far side of the bed, the quilts and counterpane pulled up and over one shoulder as she leaned on the opposite elbow. She used her free hand to pat the space closest to where Adonis stood. "You can sit here and lean against the headboard if you'd like," she suggested, silently cursing her body for reacting as it did just then to the presence of a beautiful male only inches away.

"Much obliged, my lady," he murmured as he settled against the headboard, a pillow stuffed behind his back. The padded headboard provided a head rest when he allowed his head to drop back.

His gaze swept around the interior of the canopied and curtained bed, the dim light from the fire barely illuminating the rich velvets and brocades. The fabrics weren't feminine in the least, and yet the rest of the bedchamber was decorated in a manner that suggested it could only be the mistress suite. "Are you warm enough?" he whispered.

I am now, Lydia nearly answered as she inhaled the scent of his cologne mixed with a hint of musk. "I'm fine. You're the one that's been freezing every night in front of the window," she accused with an arched brow.

"I have suffered nights far worse, my lady."

Lydia considered his response. "No doubt. But I don't want you to suffer on my account. Not any longer. Because of something Jasper made you promise a year ago," she spoke in a low voice.

"Truth be told, I'm rather glad to do it. Especially since I find myself with no other avocation at the moment." His words sounded almost sad, as if he were convinced he would no longer have a position with the Foreign Office. Oliver Preston was in custody and would probably end up transported for treason, if not hung.

"It's true there isn't a lot for Chamberlain's men to do these days," Lydia agreed. "But—"

"There are smuggling rings that need to be infiltrated. Illegal liquor trading and rum running are rampant. There are threats on Prinny's life—"

"None of which you are suited to do," Lydia interrupted in a quiet voice, rather stunned to hear his rant. Perhaps it was because they had solved the final puzzle earlier that night—she had come to realize Oliver must have been the final puzzle Chamberlain mentioned in his first puzzle—she decided Adonis was rather intelligent. Well aware of the issues that plagued England. Or perhaps it was because the man seemed entirely in the moment— not about to retreat into his head and stare into space for the next ten or twenty minutes—that she thought Adonis perfectly sane.

Adonis frowned, his gaze changing as he regarded Lydia for a long moment. "Why ever not?" he whispered, straightening against the headboard. *Christ, my own bed isn't this comfortable, and I'm not even lying down!*

Lydia allowed a sound of amusement, the soft giggle forcing Adonis to readjust his position on the bed. He hadn't been aware of how his body had been responding. He was far too close to a woman clad only in a chemise and stockings.

The three or four quilts didn't count just then.

"You are a beautiful man, Sir Donald—"

"Adonis," he interrupted. At her arched eyebrow, he added, "I rather like the way you say my name. As if you actually believe there might have been a Greek god named Adonis," he murmured. He was well aware of how his neck and face were probably coloring up just then, but in the dim light from the fireplace, he rather doubted his sudden embarrassment would be noticed.

She thinks me beautiful. Beautiful in appearance? Or ...

"Why, Adonis Truscott, I do believe you are blushing," Lydia accused, leaning forward so she could better see him. "Surely you've been told you are beautiful before," she whispered. "By a lady of the evening, or a lover? Your mistress, perhaps?"

Adonis shook his head. "No, milady," he insisted, trying with all his might to keep thoughts of Johanna from his mind just then. "I've never had a mistress, and you are the first to put voice to such a claim."

Lydia stared at him for several seconds, stunned by his comment. At first, she didn't believe him, but his manner had her realizing he had no reason to lie. "No wonder you spend your evenings in my bedchamber," she whispered. "You've no place else to be."

Stiffening at her words, Adonis was about to put voice to a protest when he had to admit she was right. He had a bed in his bachelor quarters in Green Street, but he had no desire to sleep there. He could spend an evening at Lucy Gibbon's brothel in Covent Garden—he would be in good company, no doubt, given the number of gentlemen who patronized the place—but he had no desire to share a woman.

"Don't you dare," Lydia said suddenly.

Adonis turned to stare at her. "Dare... what?" he countered.

"Go off to somewhere else. Some... *when* else," she warned in a low voice.

Swallowing, Adonis shook his head. "I assure you, my lady, I am not going anywhere. Do you honestly think I would take leave of my senses to spend time somewhere else when I am in your company?" he asked in alarm. The question was meant to be rhetorical, but Lydia lifted herself by straightening her arm and leaned in his direction, so close their bodies nearly touched.

"You did so whilst we were at the Serpentine," she accused.

Adonis wasn't quite sure what possessed him to do what he did next, but he did not regret it. For he leaned over, reached an arm around Lydia's middle, and pulled her up and onto his body, her knees forced to straddle his body, her chemise hitched up so her naked quim was pressed against the arousal behind his satin breeches.

Lydia allowed a sound of startlement when she was suddenly out from under the quilts and atop Adonis. She should have felt chilled by the sudden loss of the covers, but instead she felt rather warm. Hot, even. For Adonis captured her lips in a kiss that was nothing like the one they had shared during the garden party. Nothing like the one she had bestowed on him. Nothing like the ones in the theatre, and certainly nothing like the soft ones meant to calm her after Oliver's capture. This one was possessive. Unforgiving. Unforgettable. The entire time, she was aware of how his body reacted beneath her. Of his arousal behind the placket of his breeches pressing into her despite the barrier of his breeches.

Her fingers fumbled to find the fastenings. To tear them away, if necessary. To release the flap of fabric and allow his turgid manhood to spring forth so that she might impale herself. Perhaps Adonis would be the one who could see to a blessed release. To see to it she experienced what she had only read about in French novels or heard about in whispers in parlors. She didn't want the sharp, almost painful shards of pleasure Jasper had her experiencing just before he plunged himself into her. She wanted the waves of pleasure she had imagined could happen given the attentions of an experienced lover.

The satin of his breeches chafed at the same time it reminded her of how much she desired this beautiful man.

"Make me feel something," she whispered before her lips captured his. She could feel his entire body still with her words, feel his brief hesitance, as if he wondered if he should give in to her desires. But his lips continued the kiss even as his hands moved to grip her hips and pull her harder against his arousal.

He could feel her attempt to gasp through the kiss and reveled in how easily the art of lovemaking came back to him. The knowledge of where to touch. How hard to press. How long to hold it. Johanna had taught him. Despite not understanding each other's spoken language, she had communicated with her hands, with her kisses, with her sighs, and with her body.

When Lydia pulled away from the kiss—she needed to breathe as much as he did—Adonis raised her bottom up from his lap, knowing his manhood would see to its own escape from the black satin that had him wishing he had removed his breeches prior to sitting on the bed. Slowly settling her onto his erection, her warm, wet folds as welcoming as they were tight and slick, Adonis had to close his eyes in an effort to concentrate on where he should place a thumb. On how hard to press as he sought and found her engorged womanhood.

He knew he'd found his prey when her entire body stiffened and her gasp of surprise sounded close to his ear. "I want you thoroughly pleasured, my lady," he murmured. "I will not stop until you order me to do so." He knew his words were understood when he felt her fingernails grip the back of his shoulders. He slid the hand that wasn't busy seeing to her womanhood up the side of her torso to cover a breast, her hardened nipple settling between two of his fingers. She made another sound. He knew not if it was a whimper of protest or a plea for more, but her chemise had to go. The hand that held her breast moved to grip the gathered fabric and lifted it up and away, her lips briefly having to release their hold on his so that he could remove the chemise completely from her body.

*J*asper Barrymore must have known he wouldn't be returning from this last mission. Of all the men Jasper could have sent to watch over her, Adonis seemed the most unlikely candidate. And yet, at that very moment, Lydia wondered if her late husband had known his last wishes would best be carried out by the man who sported dashing good looks and a broken body.

If Jasper thought she would accept the man's annoying nocturnal visits because she felt sorry for the knight, then he was sorely mistaken. But if Jasper had thought to challenge both Adonis and her with an unsolvable puzzle—each other—then he had certainly succeeded. Perhaps he thought their shared avocation would give them common ground despite their differences. Perhaps it had nothing to do with their work for Chamberlain at all, but something else.

Lydia was considering the "something else" when one of Adonis' thumbs happened to stroke a particularly sensitive spot. Inhaling sharply, she nearly jerked from his hold. The steel band of one arm held her hips, though, whilst the other hand was suddenly the source of all her pleasure. Well, that and his member driven deep inside her. Despite the amount of time that had passed since he claimed her, his cock was still rock hard. Yet he hadn't moved, hadn't insisted she lift and lower herself, or flipped her over onto the bed so that he might see to his own release. It was as if he intended to see she had climaxed not once or twice, but thrice before he would see to himself.

It was between the first and second that she saw to

removing his shirt. She'd had enough of the fine lawn and instead wanted his bare skin pressed against her breasts.

Between the second and third, she complained of the satin breeches and insisted he remove them. Perhaps he thought she was giving him an ultimatum, for he set her aside, her bent legs akimbo, before angling his body over the edge of the bed. The offending garment was off his legs in seconds. Before she could take in the sight of his bare limbs, though, Adonis had pulled her atop him again, impaled her with his throbbing manhood, bent his knees, and arranged her so her back leaned against his thighs. Her bared breasts were suddenly on full display, although she was more concerned about the wicked things his fingers and a thumb were doing in the space where their bodies met. About how she was sure she was about to plunge over the edge of something very tall at any moment. Plunge and fall free.

And then she did.

Her head fell back onto his knees as a strangled cry left her lips.

At no point had she thought Adonis capable of bringing her to such ecstasy, of practicing such patience and such fierce determination to see to it she was pleasured beyond anything she had experienced before. His ministrations had her seeking his body, seeking something to hold onto in the maelstrom that suggested it might continue well into the night.

When his lips and teeth latched onto one nipple, she reflexively jerked away from him. His manhood nearly left her body before she settled back onto it. No sooner had she come down when he kissed the other nipple. Her body jerked up in response, her breath catching at the unexpected assault. When she felt more than heard his guttural reaction, she understood what she could do to see to his completion. Lifting and lowering herself, she reveled as she watched Adonis give up the control he had managed to maintain the entire time he had been in her bed.

His hands moved to grip her hips, guiding and finally

helping her until his entire body suddenly stilled and his breath caught. His face contorted and the muscles of his arms bunched the very moment before Lydia felt a wash of warmth settle into her lower body. The same moment her own body seemed to bloom with exquisite pleasure.

Whimpering and gasping for air, she slowly settled atop Adonis' body, aware of how his hands guided her down until she was securely atop him and her head ended up on one of his shoulders.

Allowing a deep breath, Adonis kissed her forehead, closed his eyes, and drifted off to a peaceful sleep.

Lydia sighed quietly, rather stunned over what had just happened. *No wonder some wives wanted to sleep with their husbands,* she thought. *No wonder widows sought a bedmate during their mourning period.*

What have I been missing? she wondered in dismay. Had her husband really been that poor a lover? And Oliver, too? She shook the thought of Oliver from her mind, not wanting to give the rake a moment more of her thoughts. But Adonis? He had spent the last hour worshipping her body at the same time he coaxed every ounce of pleasure from her. He had been unselfish, caring...

Loving.

The thought brought her up short, but at the same time something tugged in her chest.

Had Jasper thought the man capable of replacing him? In her bed as well as in her heart?

Or had he even thought that far ahead that day on the battlefield?

The afterglow of their lovemaking kept her warm for a time, but soon she sought the cover of quilts. She managed to pull several over her bare back and most of Adonis. The bit of exertion and the late hour had her exhausted, though.

"May I stay here?"

The whisper sounded loud, and if she'd had the strength, Lydia would have lifted her head to regard Adonis with a look that suggested he was insane to ask. Instead, she said,

"Of course. Besides, you must. I'm not about to move from where I am."

Beneath her body, she felt the burble of a chuckle make its way to his throat. "Good night, my lady," he whispered.

"Good night, Adonis," she murmured and finally closed her eyes.

CHAPTER 27
A CONVERSATION IN THE
MIDDLE OF THE NIGHT

A few hours later
Lydia felt a heartbeat that wasn't her own. Pressed against her cheek, the pulse, strong and even, had provided a sense of comfort for hours. Now, though, its pace had increased, and she sensed the body that held it wished to move.

"Are you well, my lady?"

The whispered words had Lydia lifting her head from Adonis' chest. "I suppose I am," she replied with a sigh. At some point in her dreams, she had cried—her final tears for the loss of Jasper—but her sobs had long since ceased, her dried tears having left salty tracks in their wake. "And you?"

Adonis took a deep breath and stretched his arms over his head, rather startled to find the one that had been wrapped around Lydia's shoulder was so warm. *No wonder men spoke of women warming their beds,* he thought absently, quickly moving his arms back below the quilts that covered the bed and the soft body of warmth stretched along his left side. "I am. I admit to a bit of embarrassment, though."

Lydia lifted her head again. "Why is that?"

The beautiful man blinked the sleep from his eyes. "I truly did not mean to ever join you in your bed, my lady," he murmured. "I thought only to sit in a chair and watch over you." *Every night for the rest of my life.*

Sighing, Lydia settled her head back into the small of his shoulder, rather surprised she didn't feel the least bit of embarrassment about allowing Adonis to share her bed. He was certainly a better bedmate than Oliver, who thrashed about in his sleep and tended to cast the covers off the bed until she finally had to wake him and send him on his way.

How could I have taken him as a lover? she thought in retrospect. The specter of loneliness certainly led to poor choices at times.

Was this one of those times? Here she was, pressed up against a naked man who seemed to have lost part of his mind and yet hadn't, really. Once he took his leave of her house—it was well past dawn—half the neighborhood would think she had taken a lover.

"Thank you for telling me about Jasper."

Adonis managed a grunt in response. "I cursed him, you must know."

Lydia held her breath, not expecting the words. "Oh?"

"He forced me to make a promise he knew I would feel honor-bound to keep. If I lived," he replied in a hoarse whisper. "I suppose he knew my wounds weren't going to kill me even though I prayed for death." He paused for several seconds before continuing, rather surprised at how lucid his thoughts were just then, as if a thick fog had lifted from his brain. "Until a few days ago, I cursed the bastard every day for a year, and now..." He paused and allowed another sigh. "I feel like such a fool." His arm, once again wrapped around her shoulders, pulled her almost entirely atop his body. "How did he know, do you suppose?" he asked as the back of one knuckle traced its way down Lydia's arm.

Could a spy really have known Adonis would carry out a promise that had been wrung from him in a moment of desperation? A moment of vulnerability?

Lydia shivered as his finger traced its path and finally

settled over the back of her hand. Holding her breath a moment, she wondered what he was talking about. "Know what?" she whispered.

"That I would fall in love with you? Despite knowing there could be nothing between us?"

Closing her eyes, Lydia considered the quiet question, rather surprised at how the few words could have such a profound effect on her. Jasper knew so much more than he ever shared with her, or probably anyone, for that matter. He knew things about people. About the men in Parliament. About other aristocrats. About the royal families of Europe. He sometimes knew what she'd been thinking even before she realized it herself.

"Perhaps," she finally murmured. "He did seem to know everything." She took a deep breath and let it out, aware of how sleepy she felt before his other question finally registered. "What did you mean when you said there can be nothing between us?" Lydia lifted herself onto an elbow and turned to regard him. "What are you doing here if not to ...?"

"I didn't intend to seduce you, if that's what you're about to accuse me of doing," he whispered. Although he had seen Lydia's body completely naked in the dim light from a dying fire, paid witness to the perfect engorged nipples, plump breasts and rounded hips as she rode him to completion, he still found it difficult to tear his gaze away from her pale collarbones and the space below.

Lydia couldn't help the feeling of disappointment that settled over her just then. "Are you married?" She had asked him before and remembered his startled response—how he had nearly toppled over at her suggestion—but she thought it prudent to ask again. Especially now that he seemed entirely there, his thoughts on the here and now.

"Of course not," Adonis replied, his other arm wrapping around her shoulders to pull her down atop him so her head ended up just below his chin. He inhaled deeply, allowing the scents of orange blossom and spice to fill his nostrils. "I rather doubt there's a woman in all of London who would wish to marry an old fogey. My leg will never be... healed properly," he murmured. "I don't know that I'll ever have the full use of it."

"You have a rather limited understanding of most of the women in London," Lydia remarked, a grin tugging at the corners of her mouth. Given how beautiful he was, most women would hardly notice his limp.

"And what say you?" Adonis whispered, his words nearly swallowed up by the darkness. At some point, he had closed the bed curtains, as much for warmth as to keep his presence secret from an awakening household of servants.

"Well, I no longer find you as much of an annoyance as I once did," she hedged, her grin widening. When Adonis didn't make a sound in reply, she lifted her head, rather shocked when she realized how close her lips were to his. "But it is a bit bothersome that you're so damned beautiful." She felt a jerk beneath her body, a sign her words had some effect on the man.

"Would you have paid me any mind at all if I weren't?" he countered, his manner nearly as playful as hers.

Lydia arched an eyebrow. "As I recall, I didn't pay you any mind at all until I caught you breathing on me at the museum," she argued in a hoarse whisper.

Adonis closed his eyes and inhaled again, intoxicated by her scent. "About that. I owe you an apology. My behavior was probably most... odd," he murmured. "It was the first time I saw you up close, and I wasn't expecting you to be so gorgeous." He was about to use the word 'bewitching' again, but thought better of it. She certainly hadn't liked hearing it at the theatre.

Jerking at hearing his claim, Lydia regarded him with disbelief. "Pray tell, what were you expecting?" she asked, realizing his expectations had to have been set by anything Jasper might have told him the last night of his life.

She felt his attempt at a shrug, rather stunned when she

realized she was almost entirely atop him. She could feel his every move beneath her body, feel the warmth of his body permeate hers, feel the hard ridge of his arousal where it pressed against the top of one of her thighs.

"An older woman, certainly."

"Well, I am nearly nine-and-twenty," she countered, deciding the truth was best. Besides, something told her the man knew far more about her than she did about him. He had spent hours in Jasper's company. Who knew what Jasper had said when death was imminent?

Adonis cleared his throat. "As I said, I was expecting an older woman. We're talking about Barrymore here. I didn't know he had excellent taste in women. That you'd have a brain behind that gorgeous face, and a luscious body to go with it." He stopped speaking and seemed to concentrate on something beyond her shoulder. When Lydia's hand waved in front of his face, he blinked and returned his attention to her. "He was a spy. He had no business taking a wife." He paused and seemed to consider something for a moment. "Unless he needed you for a cover in one of his operations," he murmured, unaware of how his words would sound to her.

Stunned, Lydia stared at Adonis for several seconds before she struggled to remove her body from atop his, her murmured, "No, no, no, no," increasing in volume with each denial.

Adonis tightened his hold on her, the steel bands of his arms preventing her from leaving his body. "And now I've gone and made a cake of it," he whispered when her attempts to thrash at him finally ceased.

Tears once again traced down Lydia's cheeks. Jasper had been a viscount, and Lydia knew he had taken his seat in Parliament despite his frequent trips away from the capital. He was in the army...

Lydia sucked in a breath and swallowed a sob. Jasper had a younger brother, the man who was now the viscount. Julian had taken that seat in Parliament, rather proud to carry on a tradition that had been passed down through five generations of Barrymores. Indeed, everything about the life of an aristocrat that Jasper had eschewed or been unable to partake in due to his service to Crown and country had been adopted by his brother. *Julian should have been born first*, she thought after a moment.

Her thoughts went back to Adonis' implication that she had only become Jasper's wife because he needed a cover. It was true the man never courted her in a manner most would think normal, but it wasn't so out of the ordinary, either.

"What are you saying? That I was... part of some kind of *arrangement?*" she whispered. Then she remembered Chamberlain's explanation. Jasper needed a wife because there were rumors he might be a homosexual.

Adonis used his free hand to reach up and scrub his face before he considered how to respond. Truth be told, he knew exactly why Jasper Barrymore had taken a wife. It wasn't as if the Foreign Office forbid marriage among its ranks, but it certainly wasn't encouraged, either. With Jasper's death, Adonis knew the spy's brother would inherit the viscountcy, and having already sired two sons, Julian Barrymore had already seen to a clear line of succession. But Adonis supposed for the sake of appearances, a viscount needed to appear as if he were doing his duty with respect to his title.

And to quell the rumors.

"I cannot presume to know Barrymore's reasons, my lady, nor his orders. But I suppose he needed to make it look as if he was carrying out his duty as an aristocrat. Take a wife. Sire an heir." He allowed his words to fade when he realized they only seemed to sadden Lydia. He hugged her harder just then. "I can only assure you he went to his grave having felt affection for you. He loved you, and regretted most deeply not having told you so." He rubbed a hand over her bare back, his warm palm calming her. "I have no intention of making the same mistake, however, so I will say it again. I love you."

Weary and suddenly so tired she could barely hold up her

head, Lydia finally allowed a nod and allowed herself to settle onto his body. "I believe you. Now go back to sleep, Adonis," she murmured.

"Yes, my love," Adonis whispered, a slight smile touching his lips as he closed his eyes.

CHAPTER 28
ADONIS GETS HIS WISH

*L*ater *that morning*

"What are you drawing?" Lydia asked, pushing away the hair from her face. Bleary-eyed, she found she wasn't the least bit surprised to find Adonis still in bed next to her. She was fairly certain he was still naked as well—at least, he was from the waist up. The bed linen covered the rest of his toned body, although most of what was beneath could be discerned through relief. She dare not move the hand nearest him in the event it would come in contact with his warm skin. The man seemed to radiate warmth even when he wasn't trying to seduce her.

Half sitting, half reclining, he was leaning against the headboard, a sketchpad resting on one raised linen-covered knee. The sounds of a pencil or charcoal could be heard scratching the surface of the rough paper.

Adonis regarded her with an appreciative glance. "Good morning, gorgeous."

Lydia couldn't help the thrill that shot through her body just then. The man was incorrigible. "May I see?" she asked as she raised herself onto one elbow.

He angled the sketchpad and aimed it in her direction. "How long should the chain be, do you suppose?" he asked in a whisper.

Lydia started at the image. It was done in exactly the same style as the one that Chamberlain had on his desk, the one of Jasper's death on the battlefield. "You're the one who did the drawing Chamberlain showed me," she murmured quietly.

Adonis frowned as he turned his attention to her, the drawing forgotten. "He showed it to you?" he asked quietly. "You weren't meant to see that. It's rather... gruesome and—"

"Necessary," she interrupted. "It answered several questions I had about how my husband died. I never would have known if I hadn't seen it," she reasoned. "Thank you for documenting the scene so completely."

Adonis seemed to think on her response for a time. "You're welcome, then." Before he could get lost in thought, he pointed to the new drawing. "How long should the chain be, do you think?" he repeated. This drawing was a rendition of a naked Adonis in recline, with the lines of bone and muscle shaded in perfect relief. Lydia was reminded of the statue they had studied at the British Museum the first day she had met him.

Had it only been a week ago?

Even his genitals were depicted, although not in the manner she had first seen his.

Just last night?

That memory had her entire body shivering in response. She quickly tamped down the thought and instead concentrated on the shackle that had been added around one of the man's ankles. The last link of a short chain was attached to a ring on the shackle.

"Is he supposed to be a slave?" she asked, her brows furrowing as her gaze went from the drawing to his face. Goodness, but the resemblance was amazing. Just as he had looked at the museum when he attempted to strike the same pose as the Adonis statue, Sir Donald looked exactly the same as what appeared in the rendering.

Well, except for the shackle.

"Something like that," Adonis replied with an arched eyebrow, his manner not the least bit teasing.

Lydia blinked. "A man leg-shackled," she murmured, thinking of the drawing in a different light. "Is that supposed to be you when you're married, mayhap?" The question came out harsher than she intended, almost sarcastic in its tone.

Adonis allowed a slight shrug. "I prefer to think of him as a slave to love," he finally said, setting aside the sketchpad and charcoal. He reached over to the nightstand and captured a bath linen, wiping his hands and leaving smears of charcoal in the soft fabric.

The sound of Lydia's gasp had him returning his attention to her. "Is it really so hard for you to believe a man can have such convictions? Especially when it comes to a woman?" he asked in a whisper. He hadn't heard any of the telltale sounds of servants up and about despite the gray light of day evident in the window, and he certainly didn't want his presence to awaken anyone if they were still abed. Given the excitement of the night before and how late everyone was up due to the lawmen and their investigation, he hoped the entire household was still asleep.

Lydia heard the hurt in his words and wondered at them. "My best friend's husband only bedded her when he was drunk and otherwise ignored her. Once your sister finally gave birth to two boys, Lord Craven spent his nights at gaming hells. Lord Pettigrew lets one of Norwick's town-houses for a mistress he has kept since who-knows-when—"

"Because they are *fools*," Adonis interrupted. "They didn't marry women for whom they felt affection. For whom they felt anything but contempt." At her look of shock, he went on. "They probably had to marry. For money. Gamblers will do anything to gain an advantage. Or they did so because they were promised to someone they met when they were in their youth and had no idea how their life would be ruined by an arranged marriage. Or because they were greedy and thought to inherit the properties of their wife's family." He paused a moment, his attention on something not quite there. "Damn opportunists." He rolled his eyes and took a breath. "I apologize for cursing, my lady," he added in a hoarse whisper.

He paused a moment to allow silence to prevail, as if realizing his rant might make him sound more foolish than the men his complaints were about. "I am nothing like them, I assure you. When I marry—and I have decided I shall marry —it will be because I am truly, madly, deeply in love."

Averting her eyes for a moment—there was something rather powerful in paying witness to a man speaking his convictions with such conviction—Lydia felt an inexplicable sting of hurt. His words made it sound as if he hadn't yet found the woman with whom he was truly, madly, deeply in love, and yet he had admitted he loved her. Twice. Just hours ago, in fact.

Why, then, was he spending so much time in her company? Appearing in her bedchamber when he knew he had been absolved of his vow to do so? Bothering her in public when she had made it quite clear she wanted nothing to do with him? Or rather, pretended she didn't?

But she did.

She couldn't deny the excitement she felt when he was near. The shivers of delight she felt when his fingers barely touched her skin. The way her nipples puckered in anticipation of whatever his lips or tongue might do. The warmth that settled at the base of her spine when she imagined what he might do with his hands. The thrill of knowing he wanted her. The evidence was clear in how his manhood tented the bed linens just then. In the way his heavy-lidded eyes pinned her in place, as if he dared her to leave the bed.

Leave him.

"So you've not yet found your true love?" she ventured, her voice carefully neutral.

Adonis regarded her, his relentless gaze still holding her in place. "Haven't I?" he countered.

Suddenly breathless, Lydia inhaled sharply. His lips were on hers in an instant, effectively cutting off any chance she had of responding, of replying to his question. How would she even reply if she could? The man had her so discombobulated she hardly knew if she had feelings for him or if she were merely attracted to him because he was so damned beautiful.

The quiet moan she allowed might have interrupted the kiss, but Adonis merely angled his head differently, never giving up his hold on her. One of his hands had moved to her shoulder to pull her closer, the thumb of his other brushing over her heated skin to caress the side of her breast. The dart of pleasure had her gasping against his lips, which broke the kiss but had his lips redirected to her jaw, to her earlobe, to the hollow of her throat.

She felt one of his fingers trail ever so lightly over her collarbones and then down to a breast and around an engorged nipple. When his lips replaced his finger, Lydia gasped again. If she didn't stop him now, she never would. The rogue would once again claim her womanhood—claim her entire body—and she would be powerless to stop him. If she told him to stop now, she knew he would honor her wishes. He wasn't a libertine. But if he stopped, she would probably hate him for it.

Decisions, decisions.

She gasped again as his lips moved to kiss the top of her other breast, his warm breaths washing over her skin to at once cool and then heat it. The edge of the bed linen passed over her shoulder and down one arm, his finger continuing to guide the fabric down until a breast was bared. His lips covered it even before the chilly air could reach it, the blade of his tongue laving over it once, twice, three times as his free hand took possession of her other breast. The nipple there, already hard and ready for his ministrations, poked into the fabric between his fingers, chafing the sensitive bud.

She inhaled sharply, thinking to tell him to stop. But why? Why make him stop what she had wanted him to do ever since that day he had interrupted her visit to the museum with his ridiculous comments? Why make him stop when she knew just how much he wanted her? Why make him stop when she already knew just how breathtaking his lovemaking could be?

She moved a hand to cover the one on her breast, sliding it and the fabric of the bed linen down her other arm. Cool air puckered her nipple even more, but it was his quick kiss and the sudden scraping of his whiskers against the side of her breast that had her nearly screaming his name.

"I apologize, my lady," he murmured before returning his attention to the newly exposed breast.

Lydia managed a wan smile as she whispered, "You're forgiven, I suppose." One of her hands delved into his tousled hair, her fingernails scraping his scalp and eliciting a deep growl from him.

When one of his hands gripped the edge of the bed linen, she felt the cotton slide down the side of one leg, felt his knuckles slide along her hot skin, his thumb trailing behind. The space at the top of her thighs throbbed in anticipation. The moan she allowed seemed to spur him on, for his other hand pushed down the rest of the quilts. Just beneath the bed linen, his hand was about to slide between her thighs. She knew it and was about to put voice to a protest, but to deny him now would only leave them both frustrated and mayhap a bit angry. By sliding one leg apart from the other, she knew she was giving him an invitation he couldn't deny.

An invitation she couldn't take back. And would always and forever offer.

He was suddenly atop her, pressing first one knee and then the other between hers. She had no choice but to spread her other leg wide. She nearly let out a yelp when his mouth left her breast and ended up just beneath her swollen breasts, suckling her belly. One of his hands moved to her quim, his fingers separating the damp curls to slide between the folds of her most private place.

This wasn't at all what she expected. This was so different from how he had claimed her just a few hours ago. Nothing about last night could compare to what Adonis was doing to her with his lips and tongue and fingers and ...

"Oh!" The exclamation was out of her mouth before she realized how loud it would sound. The most exquisite pleasure had just taken hold beneath his questing thumb. She couldn't help but cry out in surprise. Cry out as she completely succumbed to his ministrations.

A chuckling briefly erupted from his throat before his lips recaptured the tender skin of her inner thigh. Before she could even think of how he had managed to move his head that low, his tongue was on a quest to replace his thumb in providing a pleasure that was sharp and precise and exquisite. The rough texture of his tongue at once scraped and soothed as it flicked across her womanhood, lessening her hold on sanity at the very same time it tightened the coil of desire he had managed to instill in her.

Damn him.

Bless him.

When the coil gave way, she exhaled as sharply as the pleasure caught her. Her entire body seemed to bow back, her chest rising from the bed even as her bottom seemed to press more deeply into the mattress. The waves of pleasure, let loose and cascading through her, had her breathing in short gasps, her murmurs of 'yes' repeating over and over until she had to pull away from him or risk fainting from the pleasure.

Adonis allowed her a moment of recovery while his lips merely trailed down the inside of her thighs. His arousal, a situation he had been able to ignore whilst he saw to her pleasure, could no longer be ignored. He wanted her. Had to have her. Claim her and make her his once again. Once again and forever.

As to whether or not he would be as welcome in her body as he was atop it, Adonis had no idea at that moment. That is, until Lydia's hands moved down his shoulders to grip him and pull him up her body. Her legs followed, wrapping about his hips until her ankles could interlock at the small of his back, essentially trapping him over her body.

She has done this before, he remembered. Perhaps not with someone who had been a considerate lover, for she obviously expected something different than he had done. But that difference might work in his favor. *She's giving herself to me*, he realized with a good deal of relief, remembering that he hadn't exactly given her the choice the first time they had made love—she had been the one to demand it of him. Even so, he was slow in how he finally claimed her. In how he pressed the length of his manhood along her honeyed folds. In how he simply rubbed himself between those same warm, wet folds until he could stand it no more and finally entered her.

He cursed his bad leg when he couldn't move the way he remembered how it was supposed to be done. Cursed again as he took a breath and ceased his movements.

Well, he had warned her. Told her no woman in London would want him. Of course, he meant for his abilities between the sheets, but she had thought his beauty trumped all. He nearly pulled himself from her body but instead merely held her beneath him.

"What's wrong?" Lydia asked between gasps for breath.

"I'm an old fogey, if you'll recall," he whispered, even as he reveled in being inside her, her tight sheath gripping him in response to his invasion.

Lydia considered his words before she realized what he meant. She lowered one of her legs to the bed and straightened it before pushing him onto his side. She followed, adjusting her bent leg so it rested on his hip. "Is this better?" she asked, nearly frantic.

Inhaling sharply at what she had done, Adonis pressed his forehead against hers. "Bless you, my lady," he whispered.

His first thrust had her entire body reacting as he might expect. In shock at the sudden invasion, her muscles clamped on him in an attempt to force his weapon from her body. But the second thrust had her welcoming him, her body opening to take the entire length of his manhood. It was his turn to express shock when his taut sac met her quim. To growl as his tumescence was gripped from all around, the tightness of the sheath at once pulling and pushing on him. He pulled himself out of her, nearly all the way before thrusting back into her wet, tight sheath. Her quim met the hilt of his sword, eliciting a gasp and a growl from them both before he repeated his movements. The pace of his thrusts increased until he feared he was pounding into her, even though she met each and every one with an equal counter thrust of her own.

The moment he knew he could no longer hold back his release, he paused to kiss Lydia on the lips. "My love," he whispered before the extreme pleasure took hold and his seed spilled into her. Stars danced before his eyes, surrounded by an inky blackness. Another moment, and he slumped into the mattress, pulling Lydia hard against the front of his body. He passed out, his last thoughts of truly, madly, deeply.

*L*ydia felt the wash of warmth fill her lower body, the only familiar sensation of the times Jasper had bedded her. Never had there been the waves of incredible pleasure deep in her body. Never had there been murmurs of love and affection. Of forevers. Of truly, madly, deeply. Never had he held her as if she were the most important woman in the world.

She used all her strength to push Adonis so his back was in the mattress, and then she straddled him, careful to be sure he was still firmly inside her.

His groan and slight grin had her lowering her lips to his. After a quick kiss, she sighed. "Since it seems you can afford a rather generous donation to a charity..."

Adonis nodded. "I can, indeed," he agreed with a nod in the pillow, his eyelids growing heavy.

Lydia was about to say something else, but angled her head at his acknowledgement. "How, pray tell?"

A grin widened on Adonis' face, but his eyes remained closed. "I come by my wealth the old-fashioned way," he whispered.

An eyebrow arched up on Lydia's forehead. "You inherited it?" she guessed, rather surprised to learn he might be a man of some means. He did dress well, and he carried a silver-topped cane, but he had worked for the Foreign Service—not exactly a source for a large paycheck.

"I did," he admitted, his eyes still closed. "But don't tell my sister. She thinks me a pauper."

Lydia considered the edict and then the comment. "I rather doubt that," she murmured, thinking Lady Craven must have had some idea of her late father's wealth, and therefore, her brother's.

Adonis shook his head in the pillow. "She thinks I gambled it all away or spent it on whores," he whispered. After a pause, he added, "But then, I never set her straight on the matter." He opened one eye. "I learned a long time ago never to cross my older sister."

Allowing a sigh—Lydia couldn't decide if she agreed with his tendency to allow Persephone to believe what she did—Lydia decided Adonis probably had his reasons. And if he didn't cross his older sister, he probably wouldn't cross her, either.

"You shall go to the Archdeacon's office in Doctors Commons on the morrow and secure a special license," Lydia whispered.

"Oh?" he replied, his eyes finally opening.

"If you wish to do this with me again—"

"I do."

"Then we will be married."

Adonis allowed a slow, wide smile to appear. "I thought you would never ask," he murmured playfully.

"It will be very difficult for me to be with you anywhere in public when I know all the debutantes are going to be tripping over themselves for a moment of your time and attention," she countered.

Adonis blinked. "Debutantes?" *What the hell is she talking about?*

Lydia giggled and lowered her head to his. "You bounder."

"Never!" he replied with a slight shake of his head. He frowned. "Unless I need to be for you."

Sobering, Lydia pressed her forehead into his. "Only for me," she replied before bestowing him with a kiss.

"Always for you," Adonis replied.

Lydia straightened her legs and settled her body atop his, her head ending up in the small of his shoulder.

Not the least bit tempted to retreat into his head, Adonis pulled the bed linens up and over their interlocked bodies. When he was sure Lydia was asleep, he closed his eyes and drifted off to sleep, imagining Lydia in a wedding gown and then in nothing at all.

CHAPTER 29
EPILOGUE

Exactly one year later
Lady Truscott awakened to the sound of a baby giggling. She couldn't help the smile that touched her lips. The musical sound was a bit unexpected given how cranky that same baby had been in the middle of the night. She almost regretted having turned down the offer of another nurse when the boy was born, given the first nurse required two days off a week to tend to an aging parent.

Turning in bed so she faced the Greek lounging chair, she watched as Jasper Grandby Truscott, wrapped in a red woolen scarf, bounced on the crook of his father's boot, his tiny hands gripping Adonis' forefingers. When he appeared about to tilt off to one side or the other, Adonis lowered his foot until the babe's two feet touched the floor, eliciting a combination of complaint and giggles from the three-month old. Once he was safely back on board the boot, though, the foot bounced again, leveraged with the help of a bent leg over the opposite knee.

"I can't imagine your leg appreciates that particular exercise," Lydia remarked from where she watched.

Adonis stopped in mid-bounce, his son hoisted nearly a foot above the Aubusson carpet. "This leg doesn't mind a bit, actually," he replied happily. "Except your son, whom I found in bed with us this morning, seems to have gained a good deal of weight. This pony won't work for much longer."

At the sound of his mother's voice, Jasper gurgled and attempted to turn in her direction.

"Your son was in bed with us because he refused to go back to sleep at three o'clock in the morning," Lydia countered, suppressing a yawn as she put voice to her gentle complaint.

Adonis plucked the boy from his perch on his boot and lifted him over his head, sending the boy into another fit of giggles. "I rather adore that sound, don't you?" Adonis asked as he slowly lowered the babe and then sent him back up again to giggle some more.

Lydia nodded. "I do," she agreed with a grin. "Are you two going to keep each other company whilst I go to Whitehall today?" she asked as she stepped out of the bed to join the men in her life on the lounging chair.

"We are. It will be warm enough for a walk, don't you suppose?"

"Finally," Lydia agreed. "What in the world do you have him wearing?" she asked as she plucked at the scarf.

"My scarf. I bought it two days before I met you," Adonis replied. "June thirteenth." He didn't add that he could hardly remember much of anything else that had happened that day, but he could certainly remember everything since the day he had met Lydia.

She stared at her husband for a moment. "You wore it to the theatre," she remembered.

"Hmm," he agreed. "Almost as warm as you, which is why I thought it might keep him cozy until we could get him into a proper gown and a blanket," he murmured as he gave up his hold on the babe when Jasper insisted he wanted to be on his mother's lap.

"What are your plans today?" Lydia asked as she positioned Jasper in her arms. The babe promptly used a chubby fist to pull down the neckline of her nightrail and latched onto a breast.

Adonis suppressed the urge to admonish the babe. *I at least ask permission first*, he thought before redirecting his attention to Lydia. "After a walk through the back gardens, we're going to pick some tulips for the hall table, and then we'll be off to meet with the Chamberlains for supper at the Crown and Anchor."

Lydia stared at her husband a moment, a bit surprised at hearing his itinerary for the day. "You're taking the baby?"

Adonis nodded. "Lady Chamberlain is coming along and insisted I bring Jasper. Says she hasn't held a babe in years and wants the experience," he added with an arched brow.

Having seen the viscountess just the day before at tea, Lydia knew exactly why the woman wanted the experience. Lydia was quite sure Caroline Fitzsimmons was with child. Given the amount of time Lydia spent at the Foreign Office, she knew Matthew Fitzsimmons hadn't yet been made aware he would be a father anytime soon. Instead, he had made mention of a plan to be gone from the Foreign Office for an entire month. He, Caroline, and their niece, Samantha, were scheduled to take a holiday to Italy in June.

Perhaps Caroline intended to tell him whilst they were in Europe.

One of Adonis' hands waved in front of her face. She glanced over at him, a grin widening as she did so.

"Where *were* you just then?" Adonis teased.

"You cannot say a word to Chamberlain about it," Lydia said as she hugged her son close, his heavy eyes suggesting he was about to go to sleep. "Promise me, my love—"

"I promise."

"I am very certain there is a baby in Lady Chamberlain's future."

Adonis' eyes widened before a smile broke out on his face. He nearly laughed before he suddenly sobered. "Dammit, my lady, but how am I supposed to keep such important intelligence from Lord Chamberlain?" he asked in astonishment. "Especially when I'm having supper with him today?"

Lydia gave a shrug. "Think of it as a *secret,* dear heart," she countered. "One only you and I are in on."

Leaning over to kiss her on the cheek, Adonis sighed. "Keeping secrets was far easier before I married," he accused. "Back then, I didn't have anyone to share them with except for Chamberlain."

Handing the sleeping babe back to him, Lydia whispered. "You can tell Jasper. He won't tell a soul," she replied with a grin.

With that, she got up to get dressed.

EXCERPT

Read on for an excerpt from the next book in "The Widows of the
Aristocracy" series

The Secret of a Viscount

Late June 6, 1818, during Lord Weatherstone's ball

"Good God, man!" David Carlington, Marquess of
Morganfield, shouted when he discovered he wasn't alone in
Lord Weatherstone's library. "You nearly frightened me to
death."

He hadn't expected to be alone—he had arranged a
liaison with his wife—but he didn't expect to find Godfrey
Thorncastle seemingly deep in his cups and ensconced in the
middle of the long divan David had planned to use as part of
his liaison.

The fellow aristocrat acknowledged the marquess'
entrance but didn't get to his feet. "I suppose I should have
put the 'Occupied' sign out on the door handle," Godfrey
replied, his voice devoid of the humor the comment
deserved. The library at Weatherstone's mansion in Park
Lane may as well have been a brothel seeing as how many
couples used it for assignations during the annual early
Season ball. One of its frequent occupants had fashioned a
rather elaborate shingle and carved the word 'Occupied'

into its face. Hung by a drapery rope from the door handle, it prevented couples from inadvertently interrupting others who might already be busy with their dalliances.

"Since you didn't, and since my marchioness is probably still in the retiring room, tell me what has you looking so glum," David encouraged as he moved to the sideboard and helped himself to the brandy. Lord Weatherstone had his servants restock the stuff several times during the ball, although they had to time their visit so it coincided with when a couple took their leave of the room, usually between dance sets.

Godfrey took a breath and let it out. "I have to get married," he claimed.

David took an experimental sip of his brandy just as the proclamation sounded. Frowning, he regarded the viscount for a moment. "Who did you ruin?" he asked in shock.

Godfrey Thorncastle wasn't a rake. He wasn't a rogue. He probably hadn't even set foot in a brothel in... Well, David wasn't sure when the viscount might have last visited such an establishment since it had been a very long time since he had frequented any of them. He was a happily married man with a marchioness who suited his carnal needs far better than any courtesan or high-flyer could do. Hearing Godfrey Thorncastle had to marry was completely unexpected.

"Oh, no one, I assure you," the viscount replied, shaking his head. "But, I have been reminded that it is my duty to sire an heir, and I am on the cusp of yet another birthday. One of those milestone birthdays, no less."

David took another sip of the brandy, deciding it was rather good. He didn't know Godfrey's age, but he figured the man had to be verging on five-and-thirty. At the moment, he actually could have passed for forty. "Have you a candidate for your viscountess?"

Looking as if he were about to cry, Godfrey nodded. "Lady Lancaster."

Having just taken another sip of his brandy, David nearly

choked. "Ariley's daughter, Elise?" Goodness! The duke's youngest daughter had to be at least...

"She's two-and-thirty," Godfrey stated, as if he already knew the marquess was doing the arithmetic in his head. "And I dearly love her."

Deciding he didn't want to take another chance at being surprised, David set his brandy balloon on a side table and took a large wing-chaired seat adjacent to the divan. He knew of Elise Burroughs Batey, of course. The lady was a vivacious creature, ash blonde and blue-eyed and every bit as comely as her older sisters, Jane, Lady Heath, and the late Lady Margaret.

She looked, in fact, much like her mother, Margaret Merriweather, had looked when she was in her early thirties. The daughter of a duke and said to have had a dowry of one-hundred-thousand pounds, Margaret enjoyed a steady stream of suitors until Henry Burroughs, Sixth Duke of Ariley, appeared at her family's country estate in Derbyshire and announced he would be making her his duchess. Margaret's brother, John, agreed the duke should marry Margaret since the man had his own fortune. As such, John was assured the duke wasn't after his sister for her dowry.

After only fifteen years of marriage, two sons and three daughters, the duke had died. His eldest son, James, was now the seventh duke. The younger son, Andrew, was a banker and a widower with three children (although given his disappearance earlier that evening with the widow, Jane Fitzpatrick, David thought perhaps a wedding was in his future). With Margaret having died in childbirth and Jane having married nearly twenty years ago, that left the widow, Elise, as the only unmarried Burroughs daughter.

"Does Lady Lancaster know of your... affections?" David asked, his brows furrowing when realized the poor man hadn't yet proposed. If he had, David was sure it would have been the on-dit of that night's ball.

Godfrey allowed a sigh. "She won't agree to a union if she doesn't think I hold her in high esteem," he said at first, but then added, "No. I have written her with my proposal, but I didn't include all the flowery language of love."

David blinked. "Have you posted said proposal?" he asked.

"Aye. Sent it this morning."

Before he asked the next obvious question, David allowed a bit of time to pass. "And did she send a response?"

Godfrey allowed a shrug. "Not yet, or if she has, I haven't yet received it, which is why you find me in this state this evening." He was about to say more. He was about to lament that he had expected to find the woman at the ball. He had hoped to at least dance with the lady. And he was about to confide in the marquess but realized Morganfield might not be the best person in which to tell his deepest, darkest secret.

ABOUT THE AUTHOR

A self-described nerd and student of history, Linda Rae spent many years as a published technical writer specializing in 3D graphics workstations, software and 3D animation (her movie credits include SHREK and SHREK 2). Getting lost in the rabbit holes of research has resulted in historical romances set in the Regency-era as well as Ancient Greece.

A fan of action-adventure movies, she can frequently be found at the local cinema. Although she no longer has any tropical fish, she follows the San Jose Sharks and makes her home in Cody, Wyoming.

For more information:
www.lindaraesande.com
Sign up for Linda Rae's newsletter:
Regency Romance with a Twist
Follow Linda Rae's blog:
Regency Romance with a Twist